AINSLEY KEATON

The Beachfront Sunsets

VINCI
BOOKS

By Ainsley Keaton

Sconset Beach

Vinci Books

vinci-books.com

Published by Vinci Books Ltd in 2025

1

Copyright © Ainsley Keaton 2022

A CIP catalogue record for this book is available from the British Library.
Paperback ISBN: 9781036703752

Chapter One

Willow

Ever since she ran into him at the Christmas party, Willow had been trying to avoid Jackson Flynn, Ava's son. So, it had been almost 5 months, and Jackson was back in Los Angeles, but he had been texting her daily at first and then weekly. Willow didn't respond to any of its texts.

She had no desire to. Jackson was dangerous for her because he was her soulmate.

He was the one who she'd been dreaming about. Literally. He'd come into her dreams, night after night, telling her he was close. Of course, how he appeared in her dreams was different from how he actually looked.

In her dreams, he was dark-headed with long hair. And he was dressed in the style of 16th Century England, with an embroidered chemise and ruffled sleeves, a snug-fitting jacket known as a doublet, hose and a codpiece.

Sometimes. Other times, he was dressed in Victorian garb, with a top hat, long coat, vest, notched collar and breeches. His face sported the signature facial hair of the day - mutton chops.

Willow's favorites were the dreams where he appeared to her in 1920s garb. Newsboy cap, three-piece suit in brown tweed, a pocket watch, cap-toe Oxfords and a bow tie.

Still other times, he was clad in fur. In those iterations, he was hairy, stooped and spoke only in guttural grunts.

Those were just some of the ways Jackson had appeared to her. There were many, many more.

In other words, she'd gone through many lives for eons. And, apparently, there was a man in every one of those lives. The same man.

Jackson.

Of course, now that he finally made his presence known in her life, she had no interest in pursuing it further. No. If there was one thing that Willow had zero interest in, it was getting involved with a man. Any man, even her soul mate, as Jackson apparently was.

She realized that, in her previous lives, she'd given away her power. Of course. She had to. When she lived in Victorian times, she was considered her husband's property and nothing more. She was born into money in that lifetime, but that money immediately became the property of her husband from the moment she said "I do." She was a witch, then, but kept that a secret lest she be persecuted. Not that it was her husband's decision for her to live such a miserable cosseted life. It wasn't. But it was society's decision, and she had to abide.

When she lived in the 1920s, she was a feminist and a writer. She was also a powerful witch who agitated for change and spoke out about injustice perpetrated against women, blacks and other minorities. However, she was also cut down by a man in that lifetime. Not by her husband - her husband, in all her lifetimes, was good, kind and just - but by a man who dragged her into an alley and stabbed her after word got around about her abilities.

As for her life in 16th Century England...she shuddered. She remembered the rope around her neck and thinking it could've been worse. She could've been burned at the stake. But it was bad enough, and she knew she was there because of men. Specifically, the men in that country during that time and their desire to control women. Especially powerful women.

She'd lived other lives, too, many of them. And, in every one of those lives, right back to her life in the cave some hundreds of thousands of years ago, she couldn't live freely, on her own terms, because of men. She was always controlled and always had to play the dutiful woman who didn't rock the boat. The one time that she didn't play that part, her life in the 1920s, she died at 22. She was getting loud and out of her societal-imposed stricture, which proved fatal.

That was why Willow had always chosen to live life in a solitary manner. On her terms. Without having to apologize for or explain anything she did. If she wanted to spend the day shopping in the historic district, she did. If she wanted to work a spell at midnight under a full moon, she did. If she wanted to spend three whole days not sleeping and feverishly working on a sculpture that demanded to be created, she did. If she wanted to spend an entire afternoon trash-binging *Real Housewives* or the Kardashians, she did.

Mainly, though, she never had to deal with negative energies that inevitably come from any kind of relationship. She never had to absorb another person's pissy mood. She never had to walk on tiptoes, desperately trying to not disturb a drunken, snoring man like her father. That happened too many times to count.

And, of course, she never had to explain what she did. Men never got it. Women usually did. She felt a sisterhood with most women and was comfortable using her gifts around most females. But men, for some reason, mainly just thought she was strange. Not that she cared what other people thought, but it was just negativity that she didn't care to deal with.

Of course, Jackson would get it if she told him what she was. Of that, she was sure. After all, she was always a witch, wise woman, or healer in all their other lifetimes together. And in all their lifetimes together, he never seemed to mind. So she knew that this iteration wouldn't mind, either.

No matter. She still wasn't going to get involved.

Her power was her power, and she wasn't going to give away even an ounce of it. She knew that Jackson would, unwittingly or not, demand some of that power. Men always did. And in this lifetime, she was never going to give it up.

Even to her soul mate.

Chapter Two

Willow

Clara Bow was the first one to haunt Willow. "Hiya, Toots," she said in her strong Brooklyn accent. "I can't tell you how glad I am to get out of that broad's space."

She was chewing gum, her fire-engine red hair sticking up in all directions, her pencil-thin brows raised playfully, and her huge brown eyes were shining, lighting up her soft round face. Her bow-shaped lips were turned up in a huge smile. She appeared to Willow in one of her slimmer phases, as her weight tended to yo-yo during her life. She was wearing a man's shirt and tie under a skirt held up with shoulder straps.

Willow simply raised an eyebrow. "Clara Bow. What are you doing here?"

Clara Bow just rolled her eyes. "Don't I wish I knew. I got stuck with that bird because she wanted me to be there."

"Who are you talking about?"

"Zelda. She always thinks she's calling the shots. I keep

telling her to buzz off, but she don't listen to me. That dame, she thinks she's just the cat's pajamas, but I just think she's a wet blanket."

"Zelda?" Willow asked.

"Fitzgerald. You know, the broad married to that F. Scott Fitzgerald guy. I got stuck with her. God knows why." She rolled her big brown eyes. "That Zelda, she just likes to talk. Talk, talk, talk, talk, talk, but she's usually not saying nothin'. Rumor has it that Scott, her hubby, made up the term flappers because she was always flapping her gums." Then she started to laugh. "I just made that up, but it sounds good."

Willow was familiar with both women. Clara Bow was one of the biggest, if not the biggest, silent start of the 1920s. She was known for several things. She was known for her sexuality, as she slept with many men indiscriminately, including Gary Cooper for a while. She was rumored to have slept with the entire USC football team in one night, but that was just a rumor. The truth was she used to hold wild all-night parties for the team, including Marion Morrison, the football player who later became a stuntman and an actor by the name of John Wayne.

She was also known for her naïveté. She would do things like show up to a fancy dinner in a nice restaurant in a bathing suit and not understand why she was out of place. She once danced with an older gentleman who was curious about her generation and was working on an article about it. She proceeded to undress him. First, she unbuttoned his shirt and then unbuttoned his pants. As his wife was there, the older gentleman had to tell her to stop. She had no idea she was doing anything wrong.

Another thing she was known for was her refreshing lack of guile. She was the same person she always was, even after becoming famous and the biggest box office star of her time. Nothing changed her and the way she looked at the world.

Hollywood judged her because of her lack of decorum and promiscuous sex life. Clara didn't care. All she wanted was to make her movies and please her fans. She grew up in the worst slums of Brooklyn with a mother who was so mentally unbalanced that she threatened her with a butcher knife several times. This led to a lifelong battle with insomnia, as Clara was always afraid to sleep because one time she woke up and saw her mother standing over her with a butcher knife. She knew how much young girls and boys from the slums looked up to her, and she never wanted to let them down.

In the end, Clara was always looking for love. She was looking for love with all the young men that she slept with and dated. She was looking for love from her fans. She was looking for love from the people she worked with, the directors and other actors, and the people behind the scenes. She wasn't much loved by her peers - too crass, common, and wild. But she was loved by people around the world, which fed her.

As for Zelda Fitzgerald, Willow was familiar with her as well. Her upbringing was much more conventional than Clara's - she was the daughter of a prominent judge in Alabama. But she was always a wild child, the kind of girl who went to a public pool and wore a nude-colored suit that made her look naked. She and Scott were toxic to each other - they drank to excess, showed up at parties on top of taxis, got kicked out of two hotels because of their drunken behavior, and trashed every place they lived in. Scott couldn't write for years because he was too busy getting drunk and partying with Zelda. The two cheated on each other, broke up many times, and Zelda always felt neglected and unloved.

In the end, Zelda died in a mental hospital after a fire swept the place. Her mental issues might've been schizophrenia or bipolar disorder. Willow suspected the latter, as the woman was always erratic.

And now, apparently, they were haunting Willow.

And Willow had no idea why.

"Okay, out with it. Why are you here?" Willow asked Clara.

"We gotta mission. We're supposed to take you to this guy named Jackson. Guess he's your soulmate, and you seem to be turning your back on the fella. You can't do that no more. So that's where I come in," Clara explained.

Jackson. Of course. Now it was making a bit of sense. Jackson was out in Los Angeles. Clara probably was also hanging out in Los Angeles, even though she spent a few years of her life on a Nevada ranch, bringing up children and being unhappily married to an actor named Rex Bell. But she ended up back in Los Angeles, where she lived until she died.

Jackson was an actor, or trying to be. Clara was also an actor. And there was one thing that was also obvious about Clara – she really wanted to help people. Specifically, she wanted to help anybody trying to break into the movie business. She was very encouraging to men and women alike who wanted to break into the business. She was known to take several young actors under her wing to give them a shot to shine.

"And how did you manage to attach yourself to Jacqueline?" Jacquelin Delacort was a client of Willow's and had recently come to visit her for some herbal remedies. Willow somehow knew that Jacqueline had something to do with all of this, but she didn't quite know how.

Claire rolled her eyes. "That was Zelda's idea. She knew Jacqueline was coming to see you and wanted to haunt her for a little while. That Jacqueline is a real dumb bell, and that boy she's sweet on is a real dew dropper. Zelda wanted to help her see that boy was no good, but I don't think it worked."

Willow nodded her head. "Dew dropper, that means -"

"A lazy dope, that's what. She's too good for that guy, but it ain't nobody's business but hers. Anyhow, when Jacqueline came to see you, that's where we got off. We were supposed to get here anyways because this was our assignment."

Willow took a deep breath. She didn't like the sound of any of this. "Okay. Let me guess. Your assignment is to nag me into going to Los Angeles to help Jackson somehow." And then she crossed her arms. "Well, I'm here to tell you, you can nag me all you want. I'm not biting."

To that, Clara rolled her eyes. "Easy now," she said between smacks of her gum. "You don't have to marry the guy. In fact, I'm sure Zelda would tell you not to because the fella she married, he was the one who kept her down. But he needs your help."

Willow relaxed just a bit. She wasn't surprised that Zelda Fitzgerald wouldn't want her to get involved with Jackson or anybody else. Zelda was never able to get out of her husband's shadow and was never able to establish any kind of a meaningful career for herself. Even the stories she wrote for different magazines back in the day were only published because her husband had either a byline to the story, or, appallingly, were published in his name alone.

That was a shame because the lady was very talented in

many ways. She was a very talented artist and writer and was so desperate to become a prima ballerina that her inability to do so might have led to her eventual mental breakdown, although Willow suspected Zelda's heavy drinking probably was more likely to have led to her mental breakdown than anything else. And Zelda undoubtedly drank much more than she should have because her husband was a raging alcoholic, and she kept up with him.

One thing was for sure - Zelda's relationship with Scott was definitely not healthy for either of them. As for Clara, it seemed she never got close enough to any man to let them break her. She ended up broken, anyhow, but it seemed that she probably inherited her mother's mental illness. She went into a sanitarium after a mental breakdown that was possibly caused by schizophrenia, possibly caused by her mother trying to kill her with a butcher knife, or possibly caused by the lifelong insomnia she suffered because of the butcher knife incident.

Clara didn't stick around the sanitarium long enough to find out. She ended up a recluse in a bungalow, haunted by memories of a schizophrenic mother who would lock Clara in a closet while the mother turned tricks, and of a father who raped her. The doctors at the sanitarium theorized that her insomnia was related to the butcher knife incident and also because Clara was afraid that her lifelong traumas would come out in her dreams, so she was afraid to sleep.

"Clara," Willow said. "I'm not doing it. I have no desire to get involved with Jackson or any other man. Besides, he apparently needs my help to get established in Hollywood, and Hollywood was so great to you." Of course, Willow was very sarcastic when she said Hollywood was great to Clara because it obviously wasn't. She was exploited by the movie industry, not paid what she was worth and not given parts that expanded her abilities. She had no control in Hollywood.

"Hollywood saved my life, you know," Clara said. "Without the movies, I probably woulda gone crazy long before I actually did. The doctors, they thought movies were my way of escaping from my reality, and I'm sure they were. People, they thought I was a dumb bell, but I wasn't. I was just messed up in the head. You would be too if your mama was in the nut farm and your daddy messed around with you."

Willow knew this about Clara, too. She'd read her biography. She was strangely compelled to do so, even though she didn't really have an interest in the 1920s and had no desire to read about a screwed-up 1920s movie icon. Ironically, she also read Zelda's biography, even though she didn't really have an interest in her, either.

Clara read her mind. "That was me, talking in your ear. That's why you read my biography and Zelda's too. We wanted you to know what you were dealing with when we showed up."

Oh, joy. "Where's Zelda now?"

"She'll catch up. She went to her house on Long Island to see who's living there now. Zelda and me, we kind of get on each other's last nerves."

That wasn't surprising. The two women were a lot alike in too many ways. Both of them exhibitionists, both seeking attention, and both mentally ill. But Clara had accomplishments in her own name and made herself a superstar. Zelda, who didn't have any major accomplishments, probably was jealous of Clara. Zelda was always jealous of women who made their own way because she always was in the shadow of her husband.

"Listen, what if I tell you to take a hike?" Willow asked.

"You're not gonna. You gotta do this. Don't even try to say you're not gonna do it because if you do, we're never going to let you alone. We're two crazy dames, and you know I never slept when I was alive, and I don't sleep much now. You won't be able to sleep, either, because both me and Zelda, we partied all night all the time, and we'll be partying in your bedroom from now on if you don't help him."

Willow immediately thought of the movie *Ghost*, with Patrick Swayze's character, Sam Wheat, haunting Whoopi Goldberg's character, Oda Mae Brown, to force her to help his love, Molly, who was played by Demi Moore. One of the things Sam did was he didn't let Oda Mae sleep, as he sat by her bed singing "I am King Henry the Eighth I am" all night long.

She could imagine Clara and Zelda having wild parties in her bedroom while she tried to sleep. Zelda, especially, knew how to party because that's all she did. But Clara was no slouch in that department, either, as she was also famous for her all-night blowouts.

Willow realized she didn't have a choice. If she ever wanted to get rid of these two, she would have to do what they said. "Okay. What exactly do I have to do for this dude?" Willow asked.

"He needs confidence, that's all. He's in Hollywood, and he's very talented. But he's not getting a lot of roles, and he's doubting himself. He needs to know he can blow the socks off that place if he wants to, but he don't know that."

Willow finally sighed. "Okay. As long as you're not trying to force me into a relationship with the guy, I guess I'll have to go along. I don't like it, but I really don't like the idea of you guys haunting me with your all-night parties every night of my life. I need my beauty rest."

Clara rolled her eyes and smacked her gum. "I never

slept. Not really. You don't need no rest, either. That's all they ever say, you gotta get your sleep. I'm here to tell you sleep is overrated. But, okay, as long as you come with us, we'll let you get your shut-eye."

And then Clara looked behind her. "Nice of you to show up, Zelda. Late as usual."

"You're a fine one to talk," Zelda Fitzgerald said to Clara.

"Listen, Toots, I made almost 60 movies in just a few years, and I was never late to the set. You never had to be nowhere. Maybe that's why you're always late now. You never had no place to be, so no way were you ever late nowhere. But you got places to be now, so you better be on time next time."

Zelda's face, such as it was, turned bright red. "She's always rubbing it in that she was a major star and I was a nobody," Zelda said to Willow.

Clara just cocked her head a little bit. "I know I bust her chops. I don't know why. I was never like that when I was alive. I never wanted to hurt no one's feelings. But Zelda, you just rub me the wrong way."

"Likewise."

Willow just looked at Zelda. Clara obviously wasn't going to take "no" for an answer, but maybe Zelda would listen to reason. "Zelda, I don't know why you and Clara so want me to help Jackson in his movie career. You and Scott didn't exactly have a great relationship in Hollywood. You know how superficial and ridiculous the place is. So why do you want me to help him so much?"

"Scott had a problem in Hollywood because he felt that writing scripts were beneath him," Zelda said. "He felt everything was beneath him, except for his novels. He was really full of himself. But that had nothing to do with me. I didn't care about being out in Hollywood, or anywhere else, for that matter. Because everywhere we went, our problems followed us, so it didn't matter if we lived in Hollywood, the south of France, Connecticut, Long Island, St. Paul, Alabama, or New York. Wherever we went, the drinking and the parties never stopped, Scott never paid attention to me, and I always felt like a failure. Hollywood was a place where I felt like an insignificant little bug, but that was true for every place I lived."

"Yeah," Clara said. "Wherever you go, there you are."

"Clara, do you think Hollywood is a place for Jackson?"

"I told ya, Hollywood was the place where I wasn't crazy. I only went loony when I left the place. Jackson, I visited him, and he's a pretty good bird. Besides, he's the bee's knees. Dreamy. And he don't have no screw loose. He's a good egg, and that's the truth. He'll do fine."

Willow finally just took a deep breath. "Well, it looks like I'm going to Hollywood."

Clara just smiled and cracked her gum. "I knew ya'd come around."

Chapter Three

Willow

The only thing for Willow to do before going to Hollywood was she had to tell Hallie what she was doing. After all, Hallie would have to hold down the fort for her while she was in California.

She explained the situation, and Hallie, perhaps not surprisingly, took it all in stride. Hallie knew, as everybody did, that Willow sometimes was haunted by ghosts she could see and hear. That was part of the curse of being sensitive and able to see beyond the veil. And, yes, she considered the ability to see and hear spirits to be a curse, not a blessing. Normal people didn't have to put up with a ghost's demands, lest they have to put up with all-night parties if they didn't do what the ghosts wanted.

"But, boy, that's fascinating for you," Hallie said with raised eyebrows. "You're going to be hanging out with the biggest silent star of the 1920s and the wife of F. Scott Fitzgerald? Color me green with envy."

Willow didn't really see it that way. To her, these two ghosts, and every ghost who had haunted her because she was supposed to do something for somebody, were nothing but a pain in the ass. She hated being directed by anybody, let alone by a being who could make her life a living hell. And one thing was for sure, Clara Bow and Zelda Fitzgerald knew about making people's lives a living hell.

"Hallie, I wish you'd have my life for just a day. If you did, you wouldn't think this was so cool. And now I have to go to Los Angeles."

Hallie nodded her head. "You're going to be helping Jackson, then?"

"Yes. For whatever reason, he needs confidence." Willow thought about the irony that she was just telling Jacqueline that she could do a spell for her to make her more of a badass. Jackson apparently needed that for himself. There was nothing else she could really do for him. It wasn't in her wheelhouse to perform a spell to get him a job, so she just had to burn some candles, gather some herbs, light some sage, chant some words, and hope that all did the trick.

After that, she was going to be done. Done with Jackson, done with Los Angeles, and hopefully done with Clara Bow and Zelda Fitzgerald.

Just then, Ava came in the door with a bouquet of wild-flowers. "My son sent this to me," she said with a look of wonder on her face. "And something told me to bring them over here for your spa because I don't think they're for me so much as I think they're for Willow. Don't ask me why I think that."

Willow looked at the bouquet, with the pink, purple, and white peonies mixed in with sunflowers and lilacs real-ized that Ava was probably correct. Peonies, sunflowers, and lilacs were her favorite flowers. She was never much of a rose girl - she always liked the flowers she could find in a field growing wild. Jackson probably meant for the bouquet to come to her because he probably had a feeling that Willow was going to be out to see him soon to help him. Not that she'd called Jackson or even told Ava what she was about to do.

"Thanks for bringing that bouquet over, Ava," Willow said. "These will look beautiful at the front desk."

Ava looked slightly dazed. "Yeah, like I said, it's really weird for my son to send me something like this. He's not a flower kind of guy, to say the very least. Anyhow, enjoy them."

"I'd like to say I'll enjoy them, but I'm not going to probably. I'm going to Los Angeles, and I don't know when I'll be back."

Hallie had a huge grin on her face. "Can I tell Ava what's going on?" she asked eagerly.

"Sure, why not?" Willow asked. "Ava might as well know about my freaky experiences too."

"Willow is now friends with Clara Bow and Zelda Fitzgerald," she said to Ava.

"Clara Bow and Zelda Fitzgerald? You mean two women who have been dead for a long time?" Ava asked.

"Yeah, isn't that exciting?" Hallie asked. "And she's going to go out to help Jackson. That's probably why he sent the flowers. He somehow knew Willow was coming out there to see him."

Ava gave Willow a strange look. "You know, I'm surprised, but not really. Why are those ghosts coming to see you?"

"Hell, I don't know why they've been assigned this wonderful thing to do to me. I only know I have to do it, or else they'll haunt me by having wild parties in my bedroom every night. And, trust me, those two girls knew how to party."

Ava took a deep breath and smiled. "You know, I'm really happy you're going to help Jackson. He really needs a boost of confidence. He's very talented, but so is every Tom, Dick, and Harry out in Los Angeles trying to get a leg up in the movie industry. He's just one more pretty face in a sea of them."

Just then, Clara Bow showed up. "Hiya, Toots," she said in her usual greeting. "You gotta get a wiggle on. Jackson gotta audition next week, and he don't think he's gotta shot. It's a big part, and you gotta give him that boost that he can do it. It's important because he's just hanging around his place, feeling sorry for himself and drinking foot juice."

"Foot juice?" Willow asked her. "What does that mean?"

"Hooch, giggle water, cheap wine," Clara said. "He's getting zozzled every night instead of studying lines. You know what, now that I think about it, that's probably why Zelda hooked me up on this. Her husband, he got blotto all the time instead of writing, and it ruined him. You're supposed to stop Jackson from doing that to himself."

Willow turned back to Hallie and Ava, who were looking at her curiously. "Yes, Clara Bow is here in this room right now. She was just telling me that your son is drinking too much. And I guess he has a big audition next week he's going to blow if he doesn't get some confidence in himself."

"And he won't get that role if he don't quit getting so soused every night," Clara said with a nod of her fire engine red head. "So come on, we gotta get going lickety-split."

Willow just raised her eyebrows and shook her head. "The things I have to put up with. I wish I wasn't born with these gifts. To say my life would be much simpler if I could just tell women like Clara Bow to take a hike and leave me alone would be an understatement."

To that, Clara took her thumb and hiked it towards the door. "Come on, don't just sit there like some kind of dumb bell. That boy knows his onions, that's for sure, but he don't know he knows his onions. That's where you come in."

"Knows his onions?" Willow asked. She would have to brush up on her 20's slang if she was going to keep up with this woman.

"He knows his stuff," Clara said. "He's really good. You have to help him see that."

Ava was wringing her hands. "Jackson is drinking a lot? That doesn't sound like him."

Just then, Zelda appeared. "I was trying to figure out why I got this assignment, but now I understand. If your man is drinking too much, and the sauce is keeping him from fulfilling his potential, then it's important that I'm involved in helping you prevent that from happening." She appeared to sigh. "I could never stop Scott from drinking. And if he wasn't drinking so much, he could've been known as the greatest writer that ever lived. Look at Ernest Hemingway - he won a Nobel Prize for literature and a Pulitzer Prize for *The Old Man and the Sea*. That should've been Scott."

Clara shook her head. "That Ernest Hemingway, he wasn't exactly dry himself. He tied one on a lot, too. But he didn't have no anchor bringing him down like Scott had. If a dame became a ball and chain for him, he just cut 'em loose."

Zelda narrowed her eyes at Clara. "I'm sick and tired of you implying that I was the reason why Scott didn't achieve his potential. As I see it, *he* was why *I* didn't attain *my* potential."

"Let's face it, you two were poison to each other," Clara said. "It would've been better if the two of you never met."

"I agree with that," Zelda said. "At any rate, I know about the sauce cutting short what you're supposed to achieve. And I've been assigned many cases where people are drinking too much when they're supposed to focus on their dreams. I don't know why I keep getting these hard-luck cases. It's like I have to keep living my nightmare over and over again. Oh, well."

Willow turned to Ava. "Yes, apparently, Jackson is drinking too much. I'm sorry to tell you that."

Ava just shook her head. "I don't like the sound of that. Jackson has always been so levelheaded. So cool about everything. But I wonder if he keeps it all bottled in. I've always thought that might be the case. I've always worried about him because I can never get into his head to see how he's feeling. He always just tells me not to worry. But now, that's what I'm going to be doing – worrying."

"Tell your buddy it's applesauce for her to worry," Clara said between the smacks of her gum.

Zelda rolled her eyes. "Clara, you have to stop using so many slang words. Nobody's going to know what you're talking about."

"Like you're so high-falutin you never used no slang," Clara shot back. "You think you're such a cupcake, but you're not."

Zelda shook her head. "Applesauce means nonsense, just in case you're wondering."

Willow was wondering that, but she got the gist of it from the context. "Ava, let me just put your mind at ease. I'm going out to give Jackson a confidence boost. And if I do, he'll get the big part he's going for next week. At least, that's kind of what I'm getting from these two bickering ghosts."

"That's right, you'll tell Jackson he can do it, and he'll believe you. And it's his destiny to get this part, so that's why we have to help you help him," Zelda said.

"Sarah's going out to Los Angeles too," Ava said. "I worry about her. She finally fell in love with somebody good, or at least he seems to be, but he doesn't have long to live. So he's going out to stay with his sister in Los Angeles to get residency there and die with dignity. I can't imagine what Sarah's going through right now. Maybe after you help Jackson, you can help Sarah get past the grief she'll feel after she goes through that."

Willow wasn't aware that this was happening to Sarah. She wasn't a part of the inner circle, even though she was pretty good friends with Hallie. Hallie hadn't told her the story of Sarah and her new beau.

But somehow, Willow knew Sarah was going to be okay. "She's going to be a new mother," Willow said. "That's what I'm getting about the situation with your sister Sarah. That's been her lifelong dream, to be a mother. I think she's going to be just fine."

Ava nodded her head. "Yeah, actually. Sarah acciden-tally married Max. Well, it wasn't really accidental, but it definitely wasn't something she did sober. But she'll be a stepmother to Max's daughter, Julia, after Max passes away. I'd ask you how you knew that, but I already know the answer to that question."

"Yeah, it's a curse. Definitely."

Clara and Zelda were now standing at the doorway, looking at Willow like they both wanted her to run out the door. "Get your plane booked and let's get out of here," Clara said. "Let's get that bird in the air."

"Okay. I'm coming, I'm coming," Willow said. "Okay, ladies, I'll see you when I get back. Whenever that's going to be. Hallie, I trust you to hold down the fort while I'm gone. Of course, we're not going to be able to book anybody for acupuncture or herbal treatments or chakra balancing or any of that, so this whole thing will cost me a pretty penny."

"Oh, cry me a river," Clara said. "You'll make the money back when you do what you're supposed to do with your fella. Now, move."

At that, Willow followed Clara and Zelda out the door.

"At least let me take you to the airport," Ava said to Willow. "If you're going to be helping my son, that's the least I can do for you."

So, Willow followed Ava into her car so that Ava could drive her to the airport. She booked a plane ticket on the way. "I'm just booking a plane ticket for myself," Willow pointedly said to Clara and Zelda. "You girls can find your own way out there."

"Don't worry, we will. Now come on, let's scram," Clara said.

Chapter Four

Sarah

Sarah returned home after her trip to Vegas with Max and looked around her house. She never thought her life was empty, especially since she got on the island and had so many good friends and became a certified sommelier.

But now, she realized it kind of was. She never got a chance to have a young person around that she could mold and help along in life. At least, she never had that privilege until she started looking after Emerson, her good friend Quinn's daughter. And now, she was going to get that chance with Julia, Max's daughter.

Max had already told Julia what happened in Vegas, and then he called Sarah to tell her that Julia wanted to meet with her that night, just the two of them. Sarah agreed, and Julia was scheduled to come over for dinner at 6 o'clock. Sarah had no idea what the young girl would say to her, so she was a little nervous.

Her life was about to change, and she had no idea what

was around the corner. Max was going to die. Max was clear that his doctors had given him very little time, only about six months, as the melanoma had spread to his lungs and brain. It was important for what he was going to do - avail himself to the California right to die law – that he was terminal.

Sarah thought it was terrible that Max had to go to California to die with dignity. To her, it should be the law in all 50 states that if a person wanted to die on their own terms, they should be able to. She didn't know why it was anybody's business how a person died. She didn't know why a person had to endure endless pain and become more feeble and sick when everybody knew what the endgame was.

She completely agreed with Max's plan. It was a good thing that California had a law where if you wanted to, you could find a doctor to prescribe the right drugs to help you die peacefully in your sleep. But it was wrong that he would have to leave his home there on Nantucket and fly across the country to Los Angeles just so he could die with dignity.

At 6 o'clock, Julia was on Sarah's doorstep. She was dressed in a hoody, a pair of jeans with holes all over them, and a pair of Chuck Taylor hightops on her feet. Her blonde hair was in a ponytail, and she didn't have on a stitch of makeup. She had a look on her face that told Sarah that the evening wouldn't be as easy as she had hoped.

"Come on in," Sarah said to the young girl. "I ordered a pizza, and it's going to be here soon."

Julia just shrugged her shoulders and followed Sarah to the back of the house, where Sarah had set up a table and chairs on her patio. "Thanks for having me," she said to Sarah. "My dad thought it was a good idea for me to talk to you about everything because I guess you're going to be my mom after my dad —"she said with a shrug of her shoulders. "You know, after my dad…"

It was obvious that Julia didn't know how to express how she felt about her father dying. She didn't have the words for it. Sarah felt it was incredibly unfair that she would have to go through this. Her mother had already died. Now her father was going to be dead, too. And then she would end up living with a woman she didn't know. Sarah's heart went out to Julia.

"Julia, how do you feel about all this?"

She shrugged her shoulders again. "I don't know. How am I supposed to feel about it? My dad is dying, and I'll be living with a perfect stranger. But it could be worse. I could be in the system, or worse than that, living with my aunt Hannah. That would be the worst thing possible."

"Why would that be so bad?" Sarah asked.

"I don't get along with that woman, and I never have. If I lived with her, she'd try to control everything I do because that's how she is. Plus, I would have to live in New York City, and I'm not doing that. So, I guess living with you will be the least bad thing for me. But I need to get to know you. That's what my dad says."

Sarah couldn't argue with that. "Yeah, we definitely need to get to know each other. I mean, Max has told me a lot about you, and of course you've been around this house with Emerson a lot. But we've never really hung out together, just you and me. So, this is good for us to have this dinner, and maybe we can bond a little."

Julia just took a deep breath. "You know, I've prayed a lot lately. My dad takes me to the synagogue every Saturday. It's always a thing we've done when we lived in DC and when we moved out here. But I've never really prayed on my own that much. I love services. I love the music, the prayers, and the feeling I get that God is listening to me. But I've been wondering lately if He has been listening to me. Because all I've wanted is for my dad to get better, but he's not. So, I've been praying lately that I don't get too sad after he dies. I need to live my life."

Sarah put her hand on Julia's shoulder. "Julia, believe it or not, I know how you feel. I lost my father when I was really young. But I was only around four years old when that happened. But I know what it's like to lose your anchor."

"Your dad was your anchor?" Julia asked.

"Yes. He was. My mother isn't exactly the easiest person to know. She's not the kind of person to dry your tears or give you a hug when you skinned your knee on the playground or when people were mean to you. She was just very cold. She's a federal judge, so her lack of warmth is good for her job, but it wasn't so good for two young girls who didn't know what was going on. And my dad, he was much kinder than my mother. He *was* the kind to dry your tears and kiss your skinned knee."

Sarah thought back to her kind father and wished she would've gotten to know him better. Her mother, Colleen, was just not maternal in any way, shape or form. To say the very least. But her father, Kenny, was the kind of father who read bedtime stories, played Chutes and Ladders and Candy Land, had dance parties with her and Ava and took them fishing. Sarah only had vague memories of all of this, but the memories were there.

Sarah wondered how different her life would've been if her father would've lived and had been around to influence her. Her mother's attitude towards her life was hands-off, to say the very least. Colleen simply wasn't available to Sarah when Sarah needed somebody to guide her. She made such a huge mistake when she quit her job in Los Angeles to follow Nolan around the world. Would she have made that mistake if her father was alive and able to talk her out of it? That was unknowable, of course.

Now Julia was going to have to wonder that herself. Julia was in danger of growing up lost and making poor decisions because she didn't have her father around to help her. That made Sarah's role much more important. Maybe Julia wouldn't have any biological parents around to help her get into college, listen to her when she had problems, and be there for her. But she would have Sarah, and Sarah would take her future role in Julia's life very seriously.

Julia nodded her head. "Yeah, you're right about my father being my anchor." And then she started to cry. "I can't imagine my life without him. All my life, it's been just the two of us. You know my mom died before I was born. How weird is that?"

Julia was referring to the fact that her mother had died of cancer before she was born. Her mother had frozen embryos before she passed away, and one of those embryos was implanted into a surrogate. So Julia had never known her mother, not even for one day. That made what was going on with Max all the more difficult for her.

Sarah took a deep breath. "Julia, there are no words I can find to make any of this better for you. But, I want you to be assured that I'll do my damnedest to ensure your life isn't uprooted." Sarah knew that one thing she would have to do was take Julia to the synagogue every Saturday, along with learning the traditions that went along with Judaism. She felt out of her depth with all of that, but it was obvious that Julia's religion was very important to her. And that religion would be Julia's anchor once her father passed.

Ava had studied a little bit on the topic of Judaism

because she discovered her father was Jewish. Ava's father was not the same as Sarah's father, which was a secret their mother hid from both of them up until recently. Ava actually knew her biological father, even if she didn't know she knew him. She had befriended James Bloch, who was a client of her firm. She and James had lunch together often, and she grew very close to the man. It wasn't until after he died that Ava discovered that James was her father. This caused a firestorm, and Ava had difficulty with this knowledge. She felt cheated because she only considered James a good friend. She never thought of him as a father because she didn't know the truth.

Julia just shrugged her shoulders and grimaced. "It is what it is, I guess. Many people have lives much worse than mine, and I have to remember that. But it doesn't make this any easier. I feel so alone."

Sarah's heart went out to the young girl. She put her arm around her and squeezed her tight. "Are there any things you want to do before we get to California?" Sarah asked. The words were not spoken, but they were understood. "Getting to California" was code for Max's death. Sarah was, in essence, asking Julia what she wanted to see and do with her father before he passed.

"I told him I wanted us to drive to California. I want to see the country with him. He agreed. He says that's a good idea. So we're going to drive out to California the long way. In fact, we're going to be going out of our way to do a few things I wanted to do with him before he dies. Go to Disney World one last time, maybe see New Orleans. Go to the Grand Canyon. I know, it seems kind of lame to want to do all these things with my dad. But I don't want to get to California too quickly."

That was understandable. Once they were in California,

everything was going to seem inevitable. Julia wanted to put off the inevitable for as long as possible, so she wanted them to drive to California and take their time doing it.

Sarah worried Max might not have the strength to get through such a long and arduous drive. Sarah herself had made the drive from California to Nantucket when she first came out to the island. It was a 50-hour drive from hell. Her mother had accompanied her on the trip, which made it somewhat better. But she wasn't looking forward to making that same trip in reverse. Yet, that was exactly what was going to happen.

"Okay," Sarah said. "I'll go along with that, of course. Whatever you want to do."

So, it was set. The trio would drive out to California the following Monday. Sarah would have to coordinate the trip with Max, of course.

Sarah wasn't looking forward to the drive, but she was looking forward to the opportunity to bond with Julia.

Chapter Five

Willow

Willow was on the plane to Los Angeles, sitting miserably in the middle seat and trying hard to ignore the incessant chattering between Clara Bow and Zelda Fitzgerald. But it was very difficult to do that.

There was one thing about Clara Bow, and that was that she didn't have much common sense. She really didn't know certain things were wrong. Like when she showed up at a fancy restaurant for dinner wearing only a bathing suit and then wondered what the big deal was. Zelda Fitzgerald didn't have much more common sense than that. After all, she was the one who, along with Scott, arrived at a party on top of a taxicab.

So the two women, especially Clara, didn't see anything wrong with talking to Willow on the plane and expecting her to answer them. Clara was getting increasingly frustrated as she tried to pepper Willow with questions and was ignored at every turn.

"Willow, I've been asking you questions, and you just won't say nothing to me," Clara whined with a pouty look on her pretty face. "Why won't you talk to me?"

"I'm sure she won't talk to us because she doesn't want everybody around her to think she's crazy. I can relate to that," Zelda said. "God knows everybody thought I was crazy, and maybe I was. But I think I was just really frustrated by my life."

"Well, she needs to talk to us. We got the information she needs about Jackson. He's got some other dame over there right now, and that's just not right."

Willow wondered idly exactly what Clara was talking about when she said "some other dame," but there was no way she was going to talk to Clara and make everybody on the plane think she was nuts. So, she continued looking at her phone and then put on earbuds to listen to music.

"Whatcha listening to?" Clara asked. "I wanna hear it. I wanna dance."

"Clara, I doubt she's listening to anything you could dance to," Zelda said. "She's not listening to ragtime or jazz music."

Clara didn't seem to care about that. She got out in the aisle and danced wildly, her legs and arms flying, her fire engine red head bobbing up and down to some imaginary music. Zelda watched her for a moment, tapping her foot. And then she, too, got up and started dancing in the aisle.

It was quite a sight when the flight attendant came through the aisle with her cart of soda pops and peanuts as the cart went right through the two ladies, who didn't seem to notice because they kept right on dancing.

Willow tried not to look in their direction. She didn't want to add fuel to the fire. But she rolled her eyes as she listened to her music.

This was going to be a long flight. To say the least.

Six hours and two dirty martinis later, the plane finally touched down. It was six hours of the two ladies constantly talking to Willow, constantly bickering amongst themselves, and a lot of dancing in the aisles. Clara kept saying she was bored and wanted to play cards with Willow. Zelda didn't exactly complain about being bored, but she clearly was. She restlessly paced the aisles and complained to Clara that there were no "handsome men for a couple of girls like us."

Willow had to admit they were right. The men on the airplane were not exactly good-looking, at least by the standards of the two women. After all, Clara dated Gary Cooper, who was, when he was young, one of the most handsome men in the world.

Then again, what if there was a handsome guy on there? What exactly would the two women be able to do about that?

Willow got an Uber and gave the driver Jackson's address. The three of them then headed to Jackson's apartment on Hollywood Boulevard. It was nighttime in Los Angeles, 10 o'clock, and the streets were hopping.

Clara was pointing at a streetwalker, and she whistled. The woman was tall and heavy, with a lot of garish makeup, sky-high heels, and was wearing a fur coat over her tiny little dress. Her hair was bigger than her skirt.

"Look at that floozy," Clara said to Willow. "A dame like that couldn't get picked up by nobody in my day."

Zelda rolled her eyes. "What do men look for in ladies these days?" she asked.

"I don't know, but I'm sure it's not what you two are thinking," Willow said. "What did men look for back then?"

"I can't speak for other men, but Scott and I fell in love with each other's words and brains," Zelda said. "When he talked to me, it was like I was looking into a mirror. I could almost think of some words, and he would say them to me. I had every boy lining up to talk to me and dance with me. I could have had my pick of handsome men, but I chose Scott because he seemed to understand me."

Clara just smacked her gum and looked out the window. "I fell in love with Gary because he was beautiful and he had a huge manhood," Clara said, referring to her affair with Gary Cooper. "But I was falling in love with a different fella every week, it seemed like. The truth is, I never fell in love with no man, not really. At least, I never fell in love with no man to where I let them control me. Nobody was ever going to control Clara."

Zelda seemed to sigh. "You were lucky that way," she said to Clara. "You never had a man try to put you in a box and try to keep you there. You never had a man steal your words and try to say they were his own. You never had a man who made you feel that you were crazy. Who stole your dreams."

Clara nudged Zelda. "Aw, Zelda, come on now. The way you're talking, Willow's not going to want to get involved with Jackson. Why would she want to get involved with a boy if she thinks he's going to put her in a box and steal away her dreams?"

"I think Jackson is a pretty good egg," Zelda said. "I've been with him in his apartment, and he doesn't seem like the kind of guy who would try to possess Willow or anybody else. I wouldn't have gotten involved with this if I didn't think that. I'm only saying that if you're not careful, you will get involved with a man who wants to steal your essence. But I don't think Jackson's going to do that."

Willow took a deep breath. "I need to remind both of you ladies that I don't have to worry about getting involved with a man who's going to steal my dreams and put me in a box, because I'm not going to get involved with Jackson. I made that clear before I came here, and I'm making it even clearer now. I'm only out here to help him. That's it. That's all."

Willow was annoyed that Clara and Zelda seemed to just assume Willow would get involved with Jackson. Whether or not he was a "good egg" was irrelevant to her. Whether or not he had some random "dame" in his apartment was also irrelevant to her. The only thing that was relevant to her was she wanted both ladies to leave her alone, so she could work her confidence spell and hightail it back to Nantucket, where she was needed by her regular spa clients who were going to be very disappointed to find that she was on "vacation" in Los Angeles.

"Whatever," Clara said with a smack of her gum. "Why you trying to deny him your love?"

Willow looked at the Uber driver, who was looking at her with curiosity. She pointed to her ear, so he would think she was talking into a Bluetooth, and he just nodded and kept driving. "Why are you trying to change the terms of our agreement?" she demanded from Clara. "I told you, over and over, I'm not interested in him."

"But he's your soul mate," Clara protested.

"Ha," Zelda said. "I thought the same thing about Scott and he about me. From the moment we met, we felt we were fated to be together. Scott even saw a psychic one time who told him I was his soul mate. And look where that got us."

Willow didn't need to press Zelda on exactly where her being Scott Fitzgerald's soulmate got her. It was nowhere good, that was for sure. Not that Willow thought the same thing about Jackson – he seemed much less intense than

Scott Fitzgerald, much less insecure, and much less of a drunk. At any rate, when she was married to him in all her other lives, he was a good partner.

But even that was beside the point. The point was that she didn't want to be hemmed in by anybody. Besides, her life was on Nantucket, and she had no interest in living in Los Angeles. There was no way he would move to Nantucket to be with her because his fate apparently was in the movies. They were two ships that would have to pass in the night, and that was how she wanted it.

The Uber car got to Jackson's apartment in the historic Gershwin Apartments. It was built in the 1920s and originally served as a hotel. It was a brick structure with fire escapes and looked like a typical 1920s building.

Clara and Zelda both were excited to tell Willow all about the place. "Scott and I got kicked out of this hotel back in the day," Zelda said. "Back when we lived in Los Angeles and Scott was writing scripts for Hollywood that he hated writing."

"And I used to come to parties here," Clara said with a big smile. "All nighters. People were making out in the hallways and everybody was drinking bathtub gin. Those were the good old days when we used to tie one on."

Willow headed to Jackson's apartment. She'd never been there before, and she was coming unannounced, so she imagined she probably wouldn't be welcome there. But that didn't matter. She knew him well enough to know that he wasn't going to kick her out. Even though the two of them had only met one time at Ava's holiday party, she knew when he looked at her that he felt the pull they had for each other. He might not have been sensitive like Willow was, so he probably didn't know exactly why he felt like he had known her forever, but Willow knew he felt that way about her.

"Just a second," Clara said. "I need to make sure he don't have no dame in there. If he has a floozy in there, we need to come back later."

Willow just rolled her eyes. She didn't really care if he had a "dame" over or not. Still, she didn't want to be rude. It was 10 o'clock, so he might be sleeping, even if he didn't have company over.

"Go ahead," Willow said, motioning towards the door. "Go on in there, make sure it's safe."

Clara went into the apartment and came right back out. "It's safe," she said. "He's just sitting there watching something. Zelda, he's watching *The Last Tycoon*, and the guy who's playing the main part is some guy who's the bee's knees." She raised her pencil-thin eyebrows and smiled. "He's as dreamy as Gary, and I thought nobody was as dreamy as Gary."

Willow was amused that Jackson was watching an adaptation of Scott's last novel, published posthumously. Like with him sending the flowers, Jackson probably had no idea why he was compelled to watch this series. Willow wouldn't have been surprised if he started watching *Z* the Amazon series based on Zelda and Scott's marriage. Or maybe had already watched it.

Willow knocked on the door.

Jackson opened it, and he didn't seem entirely surprised that she was there. In fact, it seemed like he was expecting her. "Hey," he said. "The elusive Willow. The woman who never answers texts."

Willow just nodded her head. "Dude, I'm here to do a few things for you. One of the things I have to do is burn some sage." Willow immediately felt some nasty negative energy in Jackson's apartment, which wasn't necessarily a surprise. After all, James Earl Ray, the assassin of Martin Luther King, was known to have stayed in this building when it was the St. Francis Hotel. The place had been around since 1926, so the building had a lot of history, not all of it great.

At any rate, Jackson was depressed. It was palpable. And his depression was seeping into the walls and the space around him. It was no wonder the apartment had an oppressive feel.

To her surprise, Clara and Zelda were quiet as Willow and Jackson looked at each other. It was almost as if they wanted to stand back and give the two of them space. Willow was grateful for this because she didn't want to explain to him the existence of the two ghosts. At least, not yet.

That said, she knew Jackson would be able to roll with it. She felt he wouldn't be surprised that Willow brought two interlopers with her.

"Willow, it's very nice to see you too," Jackson said. "I'm being sarcastic, of course, because you just show up at my door, and the first thing you say is you want to burn some sage. I wish the first thing you said to me was you're happy to see me and you're sorry that you never answered any of my texts."

Clara was now whispering in Willow's ear. "He's hurt. You turned your back on this fella, and he's sore about that. You better try to make nice with him, and you're blowing it."

Zelda didn't say anything because she was too busy watching what was happening on the screen. Matt Bomer, the movie star who definitely was "dreamy," as Clara had said, played the main part of studio head Monroe Stahr.

"I wasn't with Scott when he wrote this," Zelda said wistfully. "It's the only novel he wrote that wasn't based on our relationship. Every book he wrote was based on him and me, you know. Except for this one."

Zelda looked very sad. Not that Willow could blame her because, after all, *The Last Tycoon* wasn't even completed by Scott because Scott had died of a heart attack before he could finish the novel. And Zelda was correct - every single one of his novels, except *The Last Tycoon*, was based on their relationship.

Scott's first novel, *This Side of Paradise*, featured a protagonist in love with a cruel and selfish flapper who wouldn't give him the time of day because he couldn't provide for her, which was the case when Zelda and Scott first got together. Zelda was in Alabama and wouldn't marry Scott because he was poor.

His next novel, *The Beautiful and Damned*, featured a protagonist married to a selfish flapper who spent all his money while the couple partied until dawn every night. Once again, the flapper was based on Zelda, the protagonist based on him, and this novel was based on their marriage.

The Great Gatsby had a heroine, Daisy, based on Zelda, even though Daisy was much wealthier than the Fitzgeralds, and that book was based on their lives on Long Island.

The fourth novel, and the last completed one, *Tender Is The Night*, featured a protagonist who spiraled into alcoholism while his wife battled severe mental illness. This book was written while Zelda was battling her mental breakdown.

In other words, Scott was so obsessed with Zelda throughout their courtship and marriage that he always

wrote about her. Even if his portrayals of her weren't flat-
tering, which they inevitably weren't, the novels still were
centered on her. It was a sick, codependent relationship, and
Scott seemed to recognize that as he always seemed to
portray Zelda as either selfish, greedy, or mentally ill.

The Last Tycoon didn't feature Zelda at all. The love
interest in that book was based on his new love, Sheila
Graham. That book proved that Scott had moved on from
Zelda by that time, and Zelda probably knew it. It had to
hurt to see an adaptation of the one and only novel Scott
wrote that wasn't centered around Zelda. It had to hurt
even worse that the novel had a love interest based upon
somebody else.

Zelda was watching *The Last Tycoon* with tears in her
eyes. "Scott forgot about me," she said sorrowfully. "That
last book proved it. He forgot I existed."

Willow realized she was distracted by Zelda watching
the show, so she wasn't paying attention to Jackson, who was
right in front of her.

Clara actually seemed to have a bit of sympathy for
Zelda as she went over to her and put her arm around her.
"Don't worry about that rummy," she said, using the slang
for a drunken bum, which was appropriate for Scott. "You
should be happy he didn't write about you in that book
because you told me that all the other books he wrote about
you made you look like a drunk gold-digger."

"Yes, all the other books made me look like a drunk
gold-digger or crazy, but at least he was writing about me
and not somebody else. This last book is based on the
woman he loved towards the end, who wasn't me. All those
years together and he just puts me out to pasture like I
didn't even exist."

Willow was watching the two women bond with fascination. Clara seemed to have a lot of sympathy for Zelda, for once, and why shouldn't she? Clara, of all people, knew what it was like to be cast aside. After all, Hollywood cast Clara aside in the end, even if she never got close enough to a man to let a man also cast her aside.

Jackson was now snapping his fingers in front of Willow's face. "Hey, Willow, what's going on? You show up at my doorstep, simply tell me you're going to burn some sage, and then you just space out. Has anybody ever told you you're a real odd duck?"

"All the time," Willow said. "Because I *am* an odd duck, but that's an understatement." Then she narrowed her eyes. "You don't happen to sense that there's something strange about this room, do you?" Willow was trying to gauge if Jackson felt the presence of the two ghosts in the room. She wouldn't be surprised if that was the case. He probably did sense there was something off, even if he didn't quite know what that was.

"No, not really, except the room got kinda cold when you came in the door. Which is weird, but I suddenly have the need to go and get a sweater. Which I'm going to do, but I'll be right back."

Willow wasn't surprised about that. That was one of the common things people said when there were spirits around - the temperature suddenly drops because the spirits are taking the energy out of the room. She wondered if Jackson also felt the presence of Zelda and Clara, but he didn't seem to. This meant he wasn't sensitive, but maybe that wasn't a bad thing.

While Jackson was in the bedroom, apparently selecting a sweater or jacket, Willa looked over at Zelda and Clara. "You okay?" Willow asked Zelda.

Zelda just nodded her head. "I think so. It's just weird that Scott really wasn't thinking about me when he wrote his last book. I was in a mental hospital, and he didn't even care."

Jackson came back out with a sweater on. "Okay," he said with a smile on his face. "You're going to burn some sage. What is that going to do?"

"It just clears out negative energy, that's all. And I don't want to tell you this, but you have a lot of negative energy in this apartment. I understand you're going for a big part next week. I have to make sure you're in the right frame of mind that you're going to get it."

Jackson nodded his head. "Yeah. But I don't think I will. It's a part that a lot of guys are looking at. Biopics are always a coveted role because they're Oscar winners. Rami Malek as Freddy Mercury, Phillip Seymour Hoffman as Truman Capote, Geoffrey Rush as David Helfgott, Jamie Foxx as Ray Charles, F. Murray Abraham as Antonio Salieri, Jeremy Irons as Claus von Bülow, Ben Kingsley as Gandhi - they all won Oscars. And those are only the men. Lots of women have also won Oscars for biopics. So, yeah, I have a chance to really shine, and I'm damned nervous."

Just then, Zelda looked over at Willow. "Oh my goodness, I finally know why I'm involved with this. I couldn't figure it out before. I knew why Clara was asked to do this. Clara always gets involved in hard-luck actor cases. She specializes in them. But me, I had no idea why I would've been asked to do this. But I think I know now. Go ahead, ask what the part is he's going for."

Willow asked, but she already knew the answer to that question. She was surprised herself that she didn't know beforehand, because she usually was in tune about things like this. But, for whatever reason, she didn't figure this one out.

"Jackson, what part are you going for next week?"

"It's a biopic on the life of F. Scott Fitzgerald," he said. "And I'm going for the part of Scott."

Chapter Six

Sarah

After her talk with Julia, Sarah went to see Max to tell him about their talk. She really felt she had a read on young Julia after they had dinner, but she was looking forward to the trip across the country to Los Angeles with him and Julia because she really wanted to get to know her future step-daughter better.

"You're really going to like her," Max said to Sarah. "And she really seems to like you."

Sarah nodded her head. "Yeah. I hope you don't mind my saying that this is probably a little unreal for her. I mean, she understands what's going to happen, but I doubt she's fully processed it. She knows you don't have long to live, but the idea is probably abstract for her right now. After it becomes concrete, and you're no longer with us, I worry she'll break down."

Sarah had a feeling as she talked to Julia that the young girl was a bit in denial. Julia had a hard time talking about her father's impending death, but, at the same time, it seemed to Sarah that Julia was talking about living with her so matter-of-factly that it was unlikely that the young teen truly had processed what it was going to mean to live with her, a perfect stranger.

Max nodded his head. "Yeah, I'm worried about the same thing. We've been going to counseling about it, and it seems like Julia is okay with all of this, but the counselor thinks her affect is just a little too calm about the whole situation. But I'm hoping you and Julia can get to know each other enough that it's not going to seem too weird for her to live with you."

"Yeah, I guess that's the idea of this cross-country trip," Sarah said. "But I'm worried about you, too. I made the trip from Monterey to Nantucket, which was 50 hours of hell. And I was perfectly healthy during the trip. I really don't want you to make this trip if it's going to be at all uncomfortable for you."

He winked. "That's where you come in, lovely. I'll rely on you to drive for at least part of the way. And I know what you're saying, but we'll take it slow. It'll probably take a month to get out there because we'll stop at so many places along the way. You know, stay in Orlando for a few days and go to Epcot and Disney World. Drive eight hours to the west, to New Orleans, hang out there for a few days, or maybe a week. So on, and so forth. So it's not going to be us hauling ass across the country to get there as soon as possible. It'll be us taking our time and seeing the sights."

Sarah knew that that was a good plan. It sounded like they were just going to take the trip in small chunks, so it wouldn't seem like a grueling drive so much as just a series of little mini trips.

But she was still worried. "And I assume you've seen your doctor and cleared this with him or her?"

"Of course." Then he kissed her, and she lost her breath. Why, oh why, did she finally find a man who gave her butterflies and tingles, and he would die soon? It seemed that fate just wasn't fair to her.

Sarah sighed and closed her eyes. "And you're sure about the diagnosis? Your doctor is sure about it?"

"I've had three separate opinions from three different doctors," he said. "Unless they're all wrong, yes, I'm sure."

Sarah nodded her head. A part of her didn't want to have any part of this. A part of her wanted to just walk away from all of it. She wasn't in too deep - not yet. She had fallen in love with him, but she really didn't know him all that well. If she walked away right then, she might be able to salvage her heart.

But if she went on this trip with him and Julia and then on to Los Angeles, she would get more and more attached.

Still, Julia needed her. Max did too. If she walked away from this, that would mean their marriage would be annulled, and she'd presumably have no legal right to Julia. Julia might end up going with her aunt Hannah, and Julia already said that was the worst possible scenario. Sarah cared about the young girl and didn't want her to go through any more trauma than she had to.

She was just going to have to make the sacrifice of her heart.

She smiled, and Max put his arm around her. "What's on your mind?"

"I'm just looking forward to the trip out West, that's all. I lived in California for many years, and I miss it. I lived in Los Angeles for a while, so it'll be like a homecoming." And then she blinked away tears. "Of course, it's going to be difficult for Julia and me, what's going to happen out there. But we'll get through it together."

Even as she said that, however, she wasn't sure her words were true. She was telling him that she and Julie would get through it.

But would they?

Chapter Seven

Sarah

That Monday, Sarah, Julia, and Max started the first leg of their long, long, long trip. They all decided Washington DC would be the best place to stop on that first day. After all, Washington was only a 10-hour drive away from Nantucket. The plan was to stay for three or four days wherever they stopped, which would give all of them, especially Max, a few days to recuperate between the long drives.

"DC will be a great place for us to stop," Max said. "Even though we lived there for years, we didn't really do the touristy things, and I think we should do that now. You know, go to all the Smithsonians and see things like the Hope diamond, Fonzie's jacket, and dinosaur bones. Go to the Vietnam Wall and over to the Holocaust Museum."

Sarah just had to laugh. "I know. It's true that you don't really pay much attention to the city you live in until a guest comes in to visit. So I understand why you wouldn't have visited the Smithsonians and other museums while you lived there. When I lived in Los Angeles, I didn't even visit Capitol Records or the Griffith Observatory until I had people in from out of town. I never even visited any of the movie lots. But when I had people visiting from out of town, I was suddenly doing all that, including going to Universal Studios."

Max just raised his eyebrows and grinned. "That's the truth, isn't it? Although I did go to all the government buildings, except for the Supreme Court building. But maybe you never have, so we'll go ahead and do all that."

Sarah had been around the world and seen other national government buildings, but, ironically, she had never been to the government buildings in DC., but she definitely wanted to see these buildings.

So, they set out on their drive that morning at 6 o'clock. They were going to grab some lunch on the way, so they would probably arrive in Washington by early evening at the latest. They were booked to stay at The Four Seasons, as it was going to be luxury all the way on this trip. Sarah was going to drive the first leg of the trip, and then Max would take over from there.

———

10 hours later, after they took the car ferry to the mainland and then drove to DC, the trio arrived at The Four Seasons and checked into their beautiful suite. Max was a trouper during the drive and could drive his part without any problems. So they decided to go ahead and go out to eat that evening. It was a beautiful night in Washington, cool and clear with a full moon above.

The dinner was nice, and they went to bed early that evening. Julia was staying up late as she was watching something on her tablet. But Sarah and Max were exhausted, so they hit the hay early.

The next day, they hit one of the museums. There were quite a few Smithsonians, and each Smithsonian was large enough with enough things to see that it would take several days to properly see everything in just one of the museums. They started with the Museum of Natural History, as Sarah and Julia wanted to see the Hope diamond. Julia was also excited about seeing the skeleton of the T. Rex.

"I've always been terrified of the Tyrannosaurus Rex," Julia said. "Ever since I saw *Jurassic Park* when I was a kid. It was on the big screen because it was some kind of revival, and it was one of my dad's favorite movies. And that scene where the T-Rex was terrorizing the kids in the Jeep? Oh my God. I was on the edge of my seat the whole time. I really like to see things that terrify me."

Sarah felt the same way about that movie and that scene. When the dinosaur was approaching the Jeep, and all you could hear was the pounding from behind – that was probably the scariest part of the whole scene. Sarah was like a kid herself when it came to dinosaur movies, as she had seen all the *Jurassic Park* and *Jurassic World* movies. Most of them weren't very good, as their stories weren't exactly compelling, but she enjoyed them anyway because it was really cool to see dinosaurs on the big screen.

So they went to the Museum of Natural History that day and saw everything that that museum had to offer. When they got to the Hope Diamond, Julia looked at it with awe.

"I just can't imagine a diamond being this huge," she said. "And blue."

"This diamond has been around for almost 600 years and has been passed along from one place to the next.

Kings and queens have owned it, burglars and criminals have stolen it, and, apparently, a lot of people who have either worn it or owned it have died under tragic circumstances," Max said with a raise of his eyebrows. If they were sitting around a campfire, Max would've been holding a flashlight up to his face while he told the stories about the people who met their untimely end after having worn or owned the diamond. He was clearly getting a kick out of scaring Julia about the diamond's possible curse.

Julia, for her part, just rolled her eyes when Max was trying to frighten her about the diamond curse. "Dad, I know you're trying to scare me, that maybe we shouldn't even be looking at this diamond, but I don't believe in any of that stuff. There's no curse."

Max just raised his eyebrows and smiled. "No curse that you know about. All I know is that King Louis XVI owned it, and Marie Antoinette wore it, and they both lost their heads. Mu wah wah wah."

Sarah nudged him. "You're being silly," she said. "Julia, don't listen to him."

"I'm not," Julia said. "Besides, even if there was a curse, and we're tainted by it just because we all saw this diamond, what more could happen to us? I mean, seriously, my entire life has been cursed."

Sarah couldn't argue with that, even if she really wanted to. It was true. If there was anybody who seemed to be cursed, it was Julia.

Sarah put her arm around Julia, and they moved away from the diamond. After all, there was always a line of people trying to see the diamond, so it wasn't like they could just stand there and look at it for hours even if they wanted to. Which they didn't.

By the time they got out of the museum, it was around 5

o'clock. Sarah really wanted to go to the Vietnam Memorial. The wall was powerful, with all the names of the killed servicemen. Even more powerful were the things that people had left for their fallen loved ones. There were notes and pictures, poems and stories. All those young men who lost their lives for what reason? That was the most tragic aspect of that entire war. It wasn't like the servicemen could say they stopped the Nazis from taking over the world. It wasn't even like they could say they were part of a winning war. There was no real reason why they died, and this made Sarah very sad as she looked at all the names on the wall.

Every one of those names represented a boy whose family was devastated. Maybe a boy who left children behind. And for every name that was on the wall, there were many more who bore the scars of that conflict. Men who maybe were permanently disabled from the war, either physically or mentally or both. Men who probably still woke up in a cold sweat, even to this day, as they imagined the horrors they had seen in a far-off land they didn't understand.

Julia, for her part, seemed to be just as moved by the experience as Sarah. "We've studied a little bit about this war in school," she said. "But I still don't understand what it was all about."

"Nobody does," Sarah said. "I guess we were trying to keep the world safe from communism, but the Vietnam War was definitely a conflict we should never have gotten involved with. In fact, I don't think any of the wars we've gotten involved with have been justified except for World War II. World War II was definitely a justifiable war, especially in light of what we all found out about the camps after the war was over."

Julia went over to the wall and touched it. "All those

young men," she began. "All those mothers, fathers, sisters, brothers, and children, missing somebody they love. All those lives cut so short. It doesn't seem fair."

Max was standing over to the side, his hands in his pockets. He kept shaking his head. "Julia is so right. And I'm sitting there watching her, and I realize I raised a very sensitive young lady. That can cut both ways, of course. I love that she's so empathetic, but I worry so much about how she'll be after I go. I just hope she's not too sensitive for this world."

Sarah worried about that too.

"Well, it's good she has such a heart," Sarah said. "It speaks well for you and the way you've raised her. And it's much better than the alternative, people who don't care at all for their fellow man."

Max just nodded his head. "Julia will experience something similar to what the families of these servicemen killed experienced. On a much smaller scale, of course. But there will be an empty space at the table for her. There is going to be a certain sense she's going to feel that she's not going to be able to share all the milestones of her life with her parents. Her friends have their parents alive, except for Emerson, but even she has her mother alive. I just hope she doesn't feel like she's all alone in the world."

Sarah wanted to reassure him that Julia would not feel emptiness, but she knew better. Feeling empty after one's parents die was just par for the course. No matter how old you get, when you lose your parents, it's devastating. Sarah knew that when her mother died, even if Sarah was 70 years old when Colleen passed on, she was going to feel like an orphan. So she could imagine how a 13-year-old girl would feel after losing her only living parent.

Julia came over to them. There were tears in her eyes.

"Let's go get something to eat," she said. "I'm starving. And it's been so emotional just looking at this wall and thinking about the families of these men who were killed."

So the trio left and found a restaurant to eat at.

The next day was going to be the Holocaust Museum, which would be an even more emotional experience for Julia and Max. Especially since they were Jewish. Max didn't have any close relatives who had been in the Holocaust. Yet, Sarah knew that the Holocaust was an open wound for everybody of the Jewish faith. It was so abhorrent that there could be such inhumanity to a group of people for no reason whatsoever. The persecution of the Jews had been going on for long before the Holocaust, but the Holocaust was the most tragic of all the persecutions.

Yet it was very important to go to that museum and honor all the dead. It was so important to never forget what happened over there because it seemed that every generation didn't learn the lesson that it wasn't right to persecute people just because of who they are and what they believe. It wasn't right that there were still people in the world who actively hated another person just because that person was not like them somehow.

As Sarah went to bed that evening, she reflected on her emotional day with Max and Julia. She was starting to get a good read on Julia and realized she would really have her hands full with raising the young girl. Max was right – Julia being so sensitive was a double-edged sword. Her sensitivity would make her a very good person who would bend over backward to help others. Her empathetic nature was going to serve her well in life.

Yet, it was also going to mean that she would have a very hard time with Max's passing.

And Sarah was going to have to be very sensitive to that.

Chapter Eight

Ava

The next evening, Ava, Quinn, and Hallie all met for dinner at Lola's for sushi. "Ya'll, I have some news," Quinn said.

Ava braced herself. Quinn had called this emergency meeting with the ladies, but nobody knew what was on the agenda.

"What's your news?" Hallie asked her. Hallie was digging into a rainbow roll, and was sipping on sake.

Quinn rolled her eyes. "My daughter, she can't possibly stay here on this island. She's extremely frustrated with the offerings that the school has for her artistic talents. I really thought that things were going to settle in for us, but, the more time goes by, the more I realize that I'm just holding her back."

Ava put her hand on Quinn's shoulder. "So, what are you going to do?" Ava asked.

Quinn took a deep breath. "I'm going to have to move. I've been looking at schools in New York City and in Los

Angeles, performing arts schools that would be able to really nurture Emerson's talent. I'm really leaning towards Los Angeles, because I really don't want to go back to New York City. But I'm really looking into different high schools for her. I know she's only 13, but she's so advanced in her intellect and in her violin playing ability, the school I'm looking at in Los Angeles is willing to accept her if she passes the entrance exam. After all, freshmen typically start when they're 14, so she'd only be advancing a grade."

Ava felt her heart crash down to her shoes. Ever since Emerson came to live with Quinn, Ava thought this was going to be a possibility. Emerson was happy there on Nantucket, but she wasn't thriving. She was extremely bored at the high school, and there just wasn't enough opportunity for her to flourish in her violin playing. Quinn, being an interior decorator, with a great body of work behind her, could write her own ticket no matter where she went to open up a business. So Ava knew that Quinn could thrive in Los Angeles, just like she thrived in New York City, and Nantucket.

Ava took a deep breath. "That makes you and Samantha who might be moving out to Los Angeles," Ava said.

"Come again," Quinn said.

"Yeah. You know how her boyfriend, Grayson, has been working on a fantasy novel for forever?"

"Right," Hallie said. "How is that going?"

"Well, he self-published it, and it's tearing up the charts. It's his debut novel, but somehow the word has gotten out about it, and readers are really eating it up. Anyhow, he's already gotten interest from some agents in Los Angeles who want to shop the novel around and see if they can pick up some interest from somebody working for Netflix or

Hulu. The agent seems to think Grayson has a good chance of selling his novel to Hollywood. So, Samantha and Grayson might be moving out to Los Angeles soon."

Even as Ava said that, she felt an immense, immense, immense sense of sadness. Quinn was her rock, or one of them. She couldn't imagine her life without her best friend. Sarah and Hallie would still be around, of course, but it certainly wouldn't be the same. But Ava understood that Emerson came first. The girl was brilliant, both in her schoolwork and on her violin. She really had the potential to go far with her music. Quinn couldn't possibly hold her back, and that was exactly what was happening there on the island.

And Samantha was leaving, too. Ava held back the tears, because Quinn didn't need them. Quinn needed her support, and that was that.

Quinn shook her head. "I've tried to figure this out eight ways to Sunday, and I just can't. I feel like I'm going to lose her if I don't do something to make sure she lives up to her potential. I mean, not literally lose her, because she's officially my daughter, of course. But she has the potential to really slide to the dark side if her growth is stunted. I have to be sensitive to that."

Hallie was quiet. "Oh my God. I just can't imagine life without you."

Quinn's voice was light, but Ava could tell that the lightness of her voice belied the sadness in her heart. "I know. We've been the Three Amigos for as long as I can remember really. You guys have been there for me every step of the way. But, you know, Ava – your son lives out there. You have an excuse to come out to California for him, so you can swing by and visit me."

Ava took a drink of her sake. She couldn't say anything,

because if she did, she would start crying. This island was just not going to be the same without Quinn, that was for sure. They had been best friends for 20 years or so. They were a trio, and now with Sarah around, they had been a quartet. Ava imagined they would always be close. Of course, the reality was that sometimes people come into your life, and leave an imprint on your heart, and then they slip away. Not that Quinn was going to necessarily slip away. After all, there was many means of communication – emails, Zoom calls, texting, calling, etc. But it certainly wasn't going to be the same.

Ava felt an acute sense of loss, much more of an acute sense of loss than when Deacon we went back to Australia. She was sad to see Deacon go, of course. She was in love with the idea of Deacon, and she was heading towards falling in love with him as a person. But he was new to her, and he hadn't yet been woven into the fabric of her life. Quinn was a part of the fabric of her life, and she had been for two decades. Quinn's loss was going to sting much more than Deacon's.

Still, it was cumulative. Deacon had thrown her for a loop, and she was sad about him, so this loss on top of that was just going to be a little much for Ava to handle.

Quinn shook her head again. "I wish you ladies could move out there with me. I know, I know, it's going to be a big city again. I'll make new friends. But it'll never be the same. They always say that the friends you make later in life aren't usually as close as the ones you make earlier. And I truly believe that."

"I know," Hallie said. "I think that's true, too."

Ava cleared her throat. "When are you going to move?"

"For the school year. So probably in August. To tell you the truth, this is been in the works for a while. I've applied both to schools in Los Angeles and New York. I've sent in audition videos, got a portfolio together for her and went through every hoop. It looks like the LA County High School for the Arts is going to be the place we're going to end up."

Ava was surprised that Quinn knew about this for so long, and didn't tell them. Then again, she was probably trying to wait to see if she got word from the different schools before she dropped the bomb. Ava knew that Emerson was going to get into a school, no problem. After all, the little girl was a virtuoso. She had a rare genius with her violin, and any school would be lucky to have her. Ava knew that the only snag would be the fact that Emerson was a little too young to go to high school. But Ava also knew that Emerson was a genius academically, and she would definitely be advanced enough to skip a grade. Quinn was probably waiting to see if the school would accept Emerson at her young age, and apparently the school said yes.

"Okay," Ava said. "I guess it's done. We'll help you move, of course. We'll do anything to help ease the transition."

Quinn wiped away some tears. "I love you ladies. I really do."

The three ladies gave a group hug. They were all crying.

It definitely wasn't going to be the same without her.

Chapter Nine

Willow

Jackson was going for the main part in an F. Scott Fitzgerald biopic? Willow was astounded, not just because she should've seen it coming – she was a psychic, after all - but also because she was surprised Zelda had no idea.

She would have to talk to Zelda after talking to Jackson. As it was, Zelda was freaking out about it.

"You have to find out what that movie is going to be about," Zelda said. "I don't want to help him get this part, and I feel like I've been tricked into this whole thing."

"Don't worry about it, ya dumb Dora," Clara said to Zelda. "I'm sure the movie's not going to portray you as some kind of crazy broad."

"Find out what this movie will be based on," Zelda said. "Find out if it's told from Scott's perspective or mine. Find out if it's based on one of his biographies or one of mine. It's important. And I'm telling you, if this movie goes forward and it's another hit piece on me, I'll never forgive you for encouraging your man to star in it. I swear to God, I'll haunt you every day of your life, and you'll never get another wink of sleep ever again."

Willow was about ready to go off on Zelda. It was *so* not fair for Zelda to threaten her like that. Willow was already blackmailed into doing this in the first place, and she gave into the blackmail. Now here was Zelda, still putting the heat on her. As if she had some control over the movie or the script or the part Jackson was going to play in it.

Willow wanted to tell Zelda to buzz off. She had nothing to do with this project, and even if Jackson didn't get the part, somebody was going to get it, so it wasn't fair for Zelda to put these threats on her. It wasn't like she'd be able to march over to the director and tell him not to make Zelda look bad in this movie.

She hoped the project would be more like the Amazon Prime series on Zelda. That series, which was unfortunately canceled after only one season, didn't make Zelda look bad. In fact, the series was just a bit bland and didn't seem terribly accurate according to what Willow knew about the lady. In the Amazon Prime series, Zelda was always looking at Scott and his perpetually drunk buddies like she didn't want any part of the drunken antics and endless parties. It also didn't imply that Zelda was the cause of Scott's inability to write. It didn't make Zelda seem that she was a greedy spendthrift, or that she was dating other men while she was in Alabama and he was in New York trying to make his mark, or that she was anything but a loving and supportive wife.

After reading Zelda's biography, Willow thought the Amazon Prime series went out of its way to sand off Zelda's rough edges. It was possible that if the series went on, however, it wouldn't avoid some of the more unseemly aspects of her life. Like her mental breakdown, her overall disinterest in her young daughter Scotty, her affair with a French aviator, and her general role in the breakdown of their marriage.

Unfortunately, Willow couldn't say anything to Zelda about what she was thinking about. She wasn't ready to explain to Jackson about the ghosts. She had no idea how he would take a piece of news like that, and she didn't want to lay that on him so soon.

Clara Bow was getting a bit of a kick out of this entire thing. "Hey, at least people will know about you," she said. "It sounds like this might be a major movie. Your name's gonna be on everybody's lips. I wish people would still know about me like that."

"No, you don't," Zelda said. "My life has been picked apart by so many different people. Biographers for Scott and for me, book critics who see me in all of his books and how unflattering they are to my character. You don't know what it's like to know that so many people see you as being a crazy broad when you know the truth."

Willow was going to ask Zelda what the truth was, according to her, but, again, she would have to wait. As it was, all she could do was shoot various dirty looks in Zelda's general direction when Jackson wasn't looking.

Willow was sure Zelda had a different perspective from the standard one about her life and her role in Scott's writing. After all, everybody was the hero of their own story, and Zelda was no different.

"So, you have an audition for the part of Scott Fitzgerald," Willow said to Jackson. "Do you know anything about the movie? I mean, is it based on a certain biography of him?"

Willow didn't want to know the answer to that question.

If it was based on one of Scott's biographies, especially one of the ones written by men unsympathetic to Zelda, the movie could be disastrous to the ghost that was haunting her and was threatening to keep on haunting her until the day she died.

Jackson nodded his head. "It's based on all the biographies written about him," he said. "I haven't seen the script, of course, because it hasn't really been written. The movie is just in the very beginning phase. My agent got this for me, and he thought I'd be perfect for it."

"Is it going to be made for the big screen or something else?"

"It's going to be made for the big screen," he said. "It's probably going to be more of an art-house thing because I'm not sure if mass audiences are really interested in this story. But it has so many fascinating angles and different characters in it – Hemingway, Gertrude Stein, the Bankhead sisters - and they were THE Jazz Age couple if you think about it. I wonder if it might actually be a sleeper. You never know."

"Well, I really hope you get it," Willow said.

"Yeah, me too." Then he took a deep breath and looked at her. "Now, tell me again why you're here? I guess I'm not all that clear. I mean, I'm really happy you're here. To tell you the truth, I haven't been able to get you out of my mind since I met you at my mom's Christmas party."

Just what Willow didn't want to hear. Of course, she knew why he couldn't get her out of his mind. He knew she was his soulmate, just like she knew he was hers. He might not have known this on the level she did, but he knew it on some level.

"I felt you would need some kind of a confidence booster because I know you really want this part."

He nodded his head. "I do. I really do. I know, I know, chances of my winning an Oscar for this part are slim and none. A lot of people have earned Oscars for biopics, and that's true, as I told you earlier. But all those other people had a body of work before they won the Academy Award. Except for Rami Malek. He was a bit of an unknown, even if he was in a USA series for a few years before getting the part. I have no body of work, except for silly modeling jobs I've been doing here in Los Angeles. So I think I'm delusional when I imagine myself claiming that gold statuette in front of thousands of people."

"It's overrated, getting the Oscar. I mean, what has Rami Malek done since winning the Oscar? He's been in a few things, but I don't think it's opened many doors."

Jackson just looked at her. "I know. But I feel that if I can get this part, I can be on my way. I feel like I can walk through a bunch of doors if only I can nail this audition and get the part."

Zelda was whispering in Willow's ears. "Ask him about script approval. Tell him that if this movie makes me look bad, I don't want him doing it. Tell him that if I look like some kind of lunatic in this movie, or if I look like the girl who kept Scott down, that I was the reason he didn't write as much as he should have, I will haunt him the set and everybody on it. I want you to make sure that the movie treats me fairly."

Willow just shot her a look. "Jackson, do you know how Zelda will be portrayed in this movie?" Willow asked.

"No, but if it's accurate, I doubt she'll look very good. I've been spending the last week reading biographies about Scott Fitzgerald. The woman seems to me like a narcissist, to say the least. Why do you ask?"

At that, Zelda started to howl in protest. "That's not

fair!" she screamed in Willow's ear. "I'm not a narcissist. I was in love with the wrong man, and I didn't like all the parties all the time. Those parties were in New York City and were with his friends, not mine. He was the one who was an alcoholic. I was just trying to keep up with him. And of course I didn't want to marry him at first, when he was broke, because I wanted financial security just like anybody else would. I wasn't a gold digger. I was frustrated, and *he* kept *me* down. It wasn't the other way around. You have to tell him that. Tell him right now, or I'll scream some more."

Clara was just standing in the corner, not knowing what to make of Zelda's howling like a banshee. She looked somewhat amused but concerned at the same time. "Zelda, I don't blame you. I was teasing earlier when I said at least people will know your name. Truth is, I wasn't exactly sane myself. I sure wouldn't want nobody seeing me on the screen howling like a lunatic in an asylum. It's not right that people like to see other people break down like that. It makes them feel better about their own life because they're not baying at the moon, but nobody thinks about how you feel when you're like that."

Zelda was pacing around the floor like a jungle cat in a cage. Willow tried so hard not to look in her direction. She had to focus on Jackson because he would soon ask her what she was looking at, and she didn't know how to answer that question.

Willow cleared her throat. "Listen, there's another side to Zelda that maybe you haven't seen in these biographies. She was controlled by Scott. She was sucked in by him, and he gaslit her. He made her feel like she was crazy. She didn't know whether she was coming or going half the time. He plagiarized her words and made it seem that it was right that the articles she wrote for magazines were in his name. He stole her diary and used it for passages in his own books. He never encouraged her in her ballet, art, or writing. She wrote a novel about their life, and so did he at the same time, and he stole her thunder when he published his novel. He couldn't let her have even that triumph. He kept her in a box like a butterfly. If she was mentally ill, it was because of what he did to her."

Jackson just rolled his eyes. "Revisionist bullshit," he said. "The woman was a gold-digger, and she never cared about him. He might have used a few phrases she wrote in her diary and letters to him in his novels, but to call that plagiarism is a little weak. By the time she started ballet, she was too old to do anything with that career. And when she published her articles, of course they put his byline on there because otherwise, nobody would've read them. And he couldn't write because she was constantly pestering him, demanding he pay attention to her and not to his writing. All she did really well was spend his money."

Zelda was now standing in the corner, drilling holes into Jackson with her eyes. Jackson narrowed his eyes and wrapped his sweater closer around his body. "Damn, it got even colder in here just now. What's going on?" He went over to his thermostat and turned it up.

Willow didn't want to tell him that he could turn up the thermostat to 100°, and it wouldn't make any difference. Zelda was a ball of fury and was sucking all the energy out of the room with her white-hot anger. The more enraged a ghost is, the more they use the energy in the room. Once Zelda left, the room would be way too warm.

Willow looked over at Zelda.

"Why do you keep looking at the window?" Jackson asked Willow. "Are you expecting someone?"

Willow just shook her head. "Sorry. I didn't mean to not pay attention to you."

"You need to make sure this project dies," Zelda screamed at Willow. "I won't be dragged through the mud again. I won't have my grandchildren hearing about their crazy grandmother again. The whole story needs to lay in the dust."

Jackson was shaking his head as if he was hearing things. And he might have been because Zelda was screaming at the top of her lungs and her fury was palpable.

Jackson finally just shook it off. "Anyhow, I was right in the middle of watching an adaptation of Scott's last book. It's pretty good. I actually read all of his books this week, too. I've been absorbing everything about him, so I know what makes him tick." Then he sighed. "But I really don't have any hope of getting this role. This town is really cutthroat, and I don't know why I ever thought I'd make a mark."

Jackson was a very handsome guy. Tall, built, beautiful eyes, chiseled jaw-line, and a charisma about him made everybody around him feel like they were the only person in the room. But Willow knew that his looks and charm would only go so far. He had to have the goods.

Willow knew Jackson did have the goods. She'd never seen him act, but she didn't need to. Her psychic sixth sense told her he was destined for this profession. In fact, when she closed her eyes, she could sense that he was on the verge of a breakthrough.

But right now, at that moment, he was just a frustrated model and sometime waiter. He'd been in Hollywood for over six years and had managed to get an agent and snare small parts here and there but had not yet broken through. And his head was getting in the way. His head told him that the odds of his ever getting a major role were slim and none. His head told him that every Tom, Dick, and Harry was trying for the same thing as he was. Every time Jackson went to an audition, he saw nothing but a sea of other handsome young guys who looked just like him, all of them desperate to sink their teeth into anything at all.

Ava told Willow that Jackson was always a golden boy. He was always the most popular guy in school, the stud who had women dropping at his feet and had guys wanting to be his friend because they wanted to bask in his glow. But all that golden-boy background meant nothing in Hollywood.

Willow finally closed her eyes and grasped his hand. She tried to ignore the electricity shooting through her as she sat there next to him and could feel the heat coming from him. "Jackson, you just can't give up. You're meant for this."

Jackson took a deep breath. "From your lips to God's ears," he said. "At any rate, I don't really have a Plan B. That's what's so goddamn scary. If I wash out in this town, I don't know what to do with my life. I don't have a college degree. There's nothing I'm interested in learning about, so it's not like I can just go to school and learn IT or something like that. I'm not even that good of a waiter. I can continue modeling, I guess, as long as my looks don't fade. I don't enjoy that, however. I like the idea of artistic expression, and modeling doesn't exactly provide that, to say the least."

Jackson looked like a guy who was at his wit's end. He looked like a defeated guy who was panicked after looking into his future and seeing the abyss. Willow knew in her heart that he was ready to give up, which was why she was there.

"Listen, it's late, and I want you to finish your show," Willow said. "What day is your audition?"

"It's Tuesday. Tuesday is my first really big audition ever.

This is the first time I've been noticed enough that I'm reading for the lead. And I just feel like I want to throw up."

None of this sounded like Jackson, according to how Ava always described him. She always said he was laid-back, confident, and didn't sweat the small stuff or any stuff at all. This was apparently the real Jackson, laid bare for her. Underneath his cool exterior, he was as insecure as anybody else.

Ironically, this insecure quality made him suitable for the part of Scott Fitzgerald. The outside world saw Scott and Zelda as the golden couple, the beautiful people everybody wanted to get to know. After publishing his first novel, Scott became a superstar overnight. The two were everywhere in New York, showing up to all the best parties, going to all the best restaurants and speakeasies, charming everybody they met. Even Dorothy Parker, the humorist, said everybody wanted to be their friend.

Yet, behind closed doors, Scott was a frantic drunk who despaired that he had another book in him. He suffered from writer's block and drank his way through the days. It seemed that Scott was suffering from imposter syndrome – he felt that all the accolades and all the praise he was getting from the critics and the audiences weren't warranted. He was constantly afraid of failure. All of this made him miserable, but when he went out, he put on a happy party face and made everybody believe he was a golden boy who had it all.

Jackson apparently had that aspect of Scott nailed. Like Scott, Jackson was putting on a mask, a façade that was covering up the real man who was depressed and extremely insecure.

Willow just nodded her head. "Okay. I'll be staying at a hotel for a little while," she said. "I'm going to go ahead and head to my hotel room. I need some sleep. It's been a long day and a long flight over here."

Willow was making an excuse because she wanted to talk to Zelda alone. She and Zelda were going to have to come up with a plan. It was clear that Zelda wasn't going to put up with a movie that would be a hit piece on her, yet Willow had no idea how she would prevent that from happening. Nevertheless, Willow knew that if the project went through and it made Zelda look bad and Jackson was attached to it, Zelda was never going to leave Willow alone.

Jackson just looked at Willow. "I've had a lot of trouble sleeping lately," he said forlornly. "So, don't leave on my account. Don't think you're overstaying your welcome and that I needed to get to bed because I don't think I'll be getting much sleep anyhow. Maybe if I had some company, I might sleep better."

Willow understood what he was trying to say, and she didn't want any part of it. "Make a tea with chamomile, valerian, and lavender. Stay away from the melatonin. It's overrated, and it can be addictive. Get some blue-light blockers because the blue light from your television sets and your computers mess with your circadian rhythms. And you might be deficient in magnesium. Many people are, and that's a very common cause of insomnia. So you might try a magnesium supplement or put sea salt in your water."

She was giving him advice that she would give any of her clients who had the same issues. She also was adept at performing acupuncture for people with problems getting shut-eye. She knew Jackson wasn't looking for pedestrian advice on how to get to sleep but was looking for her to offer to spend the night with him. But she wasn't going to fall into that trap.

She gathered up her things and patted Jackson on the

shoulder. "I can hang out with you again before your audition if you want. Maybe you can bounce some lines off me. I'm not a very good actress, but I can give it a college try."

She realized that she just offered to possibly play the part of Zelda to Scott if he was going to bounce some lines off her before his audition. And if she did that, Zelda would lose her mind. As it was, Zelda had stopped pacing back and forth like a caged animal and was now sitting in the corner crumpled up in a fetal position and whimpering. Clara was sitting beside her, rubbing her back and making little shushing noises.

Clara was always so good about comforting people when they were down. That was one of her special talents.

"Would you really come over and help me with my lines?" Jackson anxiously asked.

"Of course. I just said I would, and I will. Now, I have to be getting out of here. Like I said, it's been a long day, and it was a long flight. I'll see you Monday, okay?"

"Okay. But what are you going to be doing between now and then? I'd love to show you around the city. We could do touristy things, or I could show you some hidden haunts. Whatever you like."

He looked like a little boy trying to please a little girl. Willow's heart started to melt just a little, but she immediately decided it wasn't in her interest to allow him to burrow into her heart.

"I'm heading up to Frisco," she said on a whim. She really wasn't going to head up to San Francisco because there wasn't anything up there she needed to do. But she had to get out of Jackson's offer some way, so she decided to lie and tell him she was going to be out of town until Monday.

He looked disappointed. "Okay. But come on over as

early on Monday as you can. I really would like you to be here to help me."

Willow just nodded her head and backed out the door. She looked over at Clara and Zelda, and Clara caught her eye and tapped Zelda's shoulder. "Come on, babe," Clara said to Zelda. "Let's go with Willow. We'll figure it out."

Willow knew Clara held out very little hope for figuring any of it out. Clara never had any power in Hollywood. She wanted to branch out of the silly movies she was being forced to make because she wanted to do something more dramatic that showed her acting range. But she was stuck in the same non-challenging roles, where she played the spunky "It Girl" character over and over again because that was the role that made her famous. She wanted to do things like play gangster molls and other dramatic roles, but the audience only wanted to see her in a certain light, and those were the only roles she was given.

So Clara knew who had the power in Hollywood, and it wasn't the actresses. Even if she wanted to haunt somebody in charge of the Scott Fitzgerald project, it wouldn't work. Just like she didn't have power in Hollywood when she was alive, she wouldn't have power in Hollywood now that she was a ghost.

Willow was just going to have to see if she could figure out a spell that could work on the project's director, producer, and scriptwriter.

But first, she'd have to figure out who was in charge of writing the script and see if she could influence him.

"Before I leave, I'd like to know who's writing the script for this project. What's his name?"

Jackson just smiled. "*Her* name is Nancy Tallow," he said. "And I have her card."

Willow just smiled. She was having trouble getting a

read on any of this stuff. She was usually spot-on about reading people and knowing what would happen in the future. But Jackson, maybe because he was her soulmate, was throwing up a protective veil that made her not see many things she should've seen. Like the fact that the screenwriter was a woman. Or like the fact that Jackson was going for a part in an F. Scott Fitzgerald biopic.

She relaxed a little bit when she learned that the screenwriter was a woman. Willow hoped she could appeal to this Nancy's feminist heart. Since this woman was a female in a man's world, Nancy probably had a feminist heart, and Willow could influence the direction the project would take.

That was the only thing Willow could do except try some spells that would influence everybody involved in the movie. But she wasn't supposed to ever take away another person's free will, so if the people involved in the movie were going to be set on a certain direction, it would be difficult for her to make it go in a different direction.

And if it went in the wrong direction, according to Zelda, Willow would never get a wink of sleep again. Because Zelda was going to haunt her.

Chapter Ten

Willow

Willow checked into her room at the Ritz Carlton, and threw her bag down on the bed and closed her eyes, exhausted. She was going to have to talk to Zelda and Clara who, to their credits, tried hard not to talk to her while she was in her Uber car on the way over. Zelda seemed like she was defeated, like all the anger that was fueling her earlier had been depleted out of her essence and there was nothing left but a hollow shell.

Clara, for her part, seemed to sense Zelda's mood, and also seemed to understand, finally, that Willow just couldn't talk to them out in the world without people thinking Willow was crazy. Willow was very happy the two ladies finally figured out they needed to just be quiet in certain situations.

"Okay, Zelda, go ahead. Let's talk about all of this."

Zelda just shook her head. "What's there to talk about? It's going to be yet another project that's going make me look like an avaricious, drunken, silly, insane woman who was responsible for the downfall of one of our greatest writers. I just don't see any way around it."

Clara looked at Willow. "She's right. Zelda's right. Men try to always make us girls look like we're screwy, like we're always looking for saps, rubes and marks we can con. Nobody cares nothing about us. You can try to tell Zelda that this movie ain't gonna make her look bad, but she don't believe it, and neither do I."

Zelda shook her head. "I can't believe that I'm actually going to try to help your man get a part in a project that's going to be something that's going to devastate me and all of my descendants. All I can say is I want you to back out of all of this, and go home. Leave Jackson alone and hope and pray he doesn't get the part. Hope and pray the entire thing sinks into the abyss, where it belongs."

Willow just took a deep breath. "Here's the thing. I don't think I can leave Jackson, at least not yet. I'm having a lot of trouble with reading him, because he's my soulmate, but I'm feeling in my bones that it's his destiny to be out here in this town and make his mark. And I also feel it's my destiny to help him do it. So if the first thing I have to do is to convince him he can get this part, and do all I can to help him get this part, I'm going to do it."

"I don't understand," Zelda whined. "You told me before we ever got involved with you that you really didn't want to help him. We had to blackmail you into coming out here. Now you're telling me you don't want to leave him high and dry? You really want to help him get the part?"

Willow closed her eyes and tried hard to get a read on the entire situation with Jackson and the Scott Fitzgerald project. She hated that there was a veil around all of it, so she was going to have to go the extra mile to know what was going to happen with all 0f it and if her intervention was going to bear fruit. She knew in her heart that Jackson was meant for Hollywood and that he was going to someday make it big. But was he meant for this project specifically, or was he meant for some other project that was just around the corner? That was one thing she didn't know. That was one thing she was going to have to meditate on to see if she could get any kind of feeling about it.

"I don't know," Willow said honestly. "I'm going to have to burn some candles, meditate, and get a sense on what I'm supposed to be doing here. In the meantime, I'm going to call the screenwriter, see if I can meet with her, and see if there's anyway I can convince her to take the project in a different direction."

Zelda just looked defeated. "Go ahead, do what you can. I don't hold out much hope for anything. During my life, it seemed that everything was against me. It seemed that no matter what I did, no matter how hard I tried, I just couldn't get traction on claiming my place in the sun. And when I was young, everything seemed so bright for me. The boys, they were lined up to dance with me. Boys who were stationed nearby would fly their planes to impress me. I was the most popular girl in town, and I had such dreams. And I had the talent to accomplish my dreams. I had the talent, and I had the drive. But it all went to nothing. And I ended up being burned in a fire that swept through my sanitarium."

She shook her head. "Nothing went right for me in my life. So why did I ever think my legacy would be any different? I'll always be just a footnote. I'll always be Scott Fitzgerald's wife, and nothing more. I'll always be known as the woman who kept Scott down, instead of being known as the woman who was kept down by Scott. And that's just how it's going to have to be."

Willow just shook her head. Zelda, just like Jackson and Zelda's husband Scott, was wearing a mask that covered up how she really felt in her life. She wasn't the high-spirited artist, writer, and ballerina that she had built up in her head. She was the sad, dispirited woman who still, until this day, was trying to figure out exactly how it was that she died in a sanitarium, forgotten by everybody. Her soulmate, Scott, was dead by the time she died, so even he couldn't be there to remember her at her funeral.

Willow now wanted to really help her. Before, she was going to try to help Zelda because she didn't want the ghost to be haunting her throughout her life. But she got the distinct impression from Zelda that Zelda was now just giving up, and she was ready to disappear from Willow's life. She no longer seemed to have any life to her spirit.

Willow knew she was going to have to do something to ensure that Zelda's story was told in the right way. Her story had to be told in a different way from the Amazon Prime series on her life. That series didn't make Zelda look bad, but it didn't really make her look like anything at all. It just showed her reacting to the world around her, not really influencing anything, and not striking out an identity that was distinct from Scott and his partying friends. It showed her in a rather bland fashion, not as the dynamic, spirited, intelligent, talented woman she was.

Willow cocked her head. "Zelda, I think there might be something I can do. Jackson told me the script hasn't been written for this project. Which means that there's a chance that maybe the producer and director for this project might be willing to take the project in a different direction. Maybe they'd be willing to take it in a direction that would be more about your distinct voice, your distinct vision, your point of view. Maybe I could write a script that would show your life and your dynamism, and would show the world that you were something more than just Scott's muse who couldn't make the grade and ended up losing her mind because of it."

Clara was now nodding her head. "Zelda, I think it's a great idea. Willow could write the script. Do you know anything about scriptwriting?"

Willow had to admit that she really didn't. At all. She was not a writer, and she never was. Yet, she had a feeling that with Zelda's help, she could maybe pull it off. And she could sell it by pointing out that showing the woman behind the man was a hot topic for novels and books, and maybe there was an audience for a fresh movie about Zelda Fitzgerald that really captured her essence. That really showed who she was, without making her seem like a bland scold or like the opposite, which was a crazy person who did all she could to ruin her husband's life.

"There's already a scriptwriter attached," Willow said.

"Zelda, go over to that dame's house, the one who's writing the script, and see if you could figure out if she's willing to give up that project," Clara said. "Maybe if you can get her to back out, and Willow could spend this entire weekend banging out another script, she can convince the people behind this movie that they should use her script instead."

Willow just rolled her eyes. "Come on, I don't have a name, and I don't have any pull in this town. I don't think anybody's going to buy a script from me."

"Maybe not, but maybe you need to talk to this Nancy broad and see how interested she is in writing this script," Clara said. "Maybe she don't really want to write it, and she'd be happy if you wrote something for her to slap her name on it and hand it in. Tell her she can have it as her own, and nobody needs to know that you were the ghost writer. I bet that'll work."

Willow closed her eyes, and realized Clara was right. She was finally starting to have a clear head about what was going on around her, and she was able to focus in on Nancy's wavelength. She was starting to realize that Clara was correct – Nancy was suffering from writer's block, she was overwhelmed and was worried she wouldn't be able to get the Fitzgerald script done on time. When she really concentrated on Nancy, that was the message that was coming through to her loud and clear.

Willow suddenly realized that she was meant to be in Los Angeles not necessarily to help Jackson, but to help Zelda. She was meant to come out there to be a ghost writer for this project. She was meant to shape the project to where it was Zelda's story that was being told, through Zelda's eyes, and not through Scott's.

She was meant to write a script that was going to be produced that was going to make the world see Zelda in a different light.

And she was going to have the best consultant for this project possible.

She was going to have Zelda herself help guide the project.

But first she was going to have to talk to Nancy and offer her services.

Chapter Eleven

Sarah

Sarah, Max and Julia went to the Holocaust Museum, which was another very emotional day for everybody. Just like Sarah thought, this was a very powerful experience for Julia and Max.

They spent a week in Washington DC, seeing the sights, looking at the cherry trees in full bloom, and even taking a boat out on the Potomac. Sarah wanted to spend as much time in Washington DC as possible to ensure that Max rested enough for another long leg of the trip.

There were a few days when Max had to stay in the hotel room as Julia and Sarah went on the town themselves. He just wasn't up to sightseeing every single day. Sarah worried about the days he was down, but these days were necessary for him because he was able to join them the next day.

Finally, it was time to move on. They all headed to Orlando, Florida, because they wanted to see Disney World and Epcot Center. Julia had never been to these places, and she always wanted to go, so Max was going to take her.

They spent two weeks in Orlando. They had a hotel with a beachfront view and spent day after day just relaxing and going to Disney World a few times. Once again, Max couldn't join them every day, but they tried to take it easy on most days. Sarah was very worried about Max being out in the sun, so they all stayed away from the actual beach, preferring to sit on the veranda and watch the waves coming in from there.

From there, they went to New Orleans and spent a week. They passed through Helen, Georgia, Quinn's hometown, and met up with Quinn on the way. Quinn had always told Sarah she needed to see that beautiful little town. It was like an old Bavarian town, with buildings reminiscent of 15th-century Bavaria. But it was a place that had wineries, zip lining, trails, and so much natural beauty.

Quinn was an amazing guide for the beautiful little place. Sarah and Julia zip-lined, hiked, and kayaked with Quinn for a weekend, while Max relaxed in a beautiful little hotel set at the foot of some hills.

New Orleans was next. By that time, Max was unable to do a lot with them. But he could go out to the French Quarter with them a couple of evenings. Those evenings were cherished by everybody because Sarah and Julia both were starting to understand that time was getting shorter and shorter.

One evening, they were sitting in a French Quarter restaurant when Max looked at Sarah. "Sarah, I need to ask you a favor. I'm really wearing out. I feel like one of those wind-up toys. When you first wind up the toy, the monkey or whatever goes really quickly. But as time goes on, he goes slower and slower and slower. And then he stops. I feel like I'm winding down."

Sarah nodded her head. She was afraid of this. She'd seen him slowly deteriorating over the course of the last few weeks. She was hesitant to even take this trip with him because she knew he was wearing out and it would be hard for him. Now, he was telling her what she already knew, and she would have to acknowledge it.

"You need to fly to Los Angeles, don't you?"

He nodded his head. "We need to figure out something. Obviously, I can't just abandon the SUV here in New Orleans. In hindsight, getting to my sister's house this way wasn't the greatest idea. But we can do nothing to turn back time and do things differently. We can only figure out a plan for how to get the SUV out to Los Angeles, so I can just fly out there and relax in my sister's home for a few months while I fill out the necessary paperwork I'm going to need to establish residency in California."

"I'll drive the car out to California," Sarah said. "You and Julia should fly ahead to Los Angeles." The SUV needed to get out to California because Max would have to register it in California as part of the process to establish residency.

"Thank you," he said to her. He grabbed her hand and looked into her eyes. "I really couldn't do this without you. I wish we would have had a lot more time together. It doesn't seem fair that I met you when there's so little time left. It seems like we should've met years ago."

Sarah just smiled and cocked her head. "Well, life isn't always fair. And I know that very well. If it makes you feel any better, I'm an old pro at driving across the country. When I came from Monterey to move to Nantucket, I drove the entire way even though my mother was next to me the whole time. So you can trust me not to wreck the car on the way out."

Sarah got an idea. Ava wasn't really doing anything. It was now the middle of April, and the island was not yet hopping with tourists, which it would be after Memorial Day in just a few weeks. That meant Ava was just hanging around her house, with a lot of downtime and boredom. She no longer had a relationship to worry about, as Deacon was still in Australia with his sister, and Ava told her ex-husband to take a hike when he tried to come back. Not only that, she still had Jessica on as a full-time employee, so even though Ava had a couple of people staying with her at any given time, Jessica took care of them.

In other words, Ava was probably looking for something to do. And she would be more than willing to fly out to New Orleans to meet Sarah and help her drive to Los Angeles. So, Sarah called Ava that evening, explained what was going on, and Ava eagerly agreed to fly out to meet her.

"Oh, God, yes," Ava said when Sarah called her and asked her if she wanted to drive with her to Los Angeles. "I can't tell you how bored I am around here," she said. "In the past few weeks, I think I've read about five books and watched about six Netflix series, and I'm Netflixed and booked out. Not that those are words, but they're appropriate for the situation."

Sarah told Max about Ava's decision, and he was relieved. "I'm happy she's going to come and help you drive out to Los Angeles. I hate to ask you to do this, but-"

"Of course. I understand. You want to spend time with your sister and your daughter and relax while doing it. And sitting in a car for 10 hours a day is the opposite of relaxation. I get it."

Sarah didn't want to tell Max she was quite happy about Ava coming to drive with her. She and Ava spent the better part of two decades not speaking to one another for various silly reasons. But they were the best of friends now, closer than two sisters could be, and Sarah knew Ava would be a great road companion for her.

Sarah hated to think the two of them would have some fun on the way, but, at the same time, she knew they would. And it was strange – she almost felt guilty that she would have a good time with Ava. It was almost like she felt obligated to feel miserable because the man she had fallen in love with didn't have much time left and, in fact, was deteriorating much more rapidly than she imagined he would.

Max seemed to read her mind. "I want you and Ava to have a good time on this road trip. Don't worry about me. Obviously, we'll talk on the phone as much as possible, but I don't want you to feel restrained because somehow it wouldn't feel right considering my situation. Above all, I need you to live your life."

Sarah nodded, but she had a huge lump in her throat. She blinked back tears. Max didn't need her tears. Max needed to go to his sister Mary's house and spend time with his sister and Julia. He needed to make the most of what little time he had left.

The next day, Max and Julia flew out to Los Angeles, and Ava flew into New Orleans. Ava gave Sarah a big hug, which was exactly what Sarah needed. Ava was her rock. Truth be told, Ava was always her rock when they were growing up. Ava never knew that, but she was. Sarah always looked up to her big sister. She still regretted the decades they didn't talk, but they were making up for lost time.

When Ava gave her that hug, the deluge of tears threatening the entire trip came tumbling out. Sarah cried on Ava's shoulder for what seemed like hours but probably was only a few minutes.

"Sarah, I'm here for you. I'll always be here for you. And I want you to know that you're not going to be raising Julia alone, any more than Quinn is raising Emerson alone. Just like we're all helping out, pitching in with Emerson, we're going to be helping out and pitching in with Julia. We're all going to be one big happy family, and Julia will have three godmothers and a mother. She's never going to have to walk alone, and neither will you."

Ava didn't need to say all these words because Sarah knew them. She knew exactly what Ava was saying to her. And she instinctively knew Ava was right. They were all going to be a family, just like they always were. Just like Ava, herself, and Hallie stepped in and helped out with Emerson's care, Ava, Hallie, and Quinn were all going to step up to the plate when it came to Julia.

"I feel so silly," Sarah said. "I mean, I barely know Max. He was my campaign advisor, but I fell in love with him, and I think I'll feel empty when he dies. There will be an ache in my heart, a hole that will be left. I just know it. I got off so easy with Nolan's death, in a way. I had long since left him emotionally when he was diagnosed with ALS, so when he died, I felt nothing but relief. It's going to be different this time. I know it."

Ava just nodded her head. "Of course it is. But you know that going in. And you're just going to have to work through it, with your sister and best friends by your side, holding your hand and giving you a shoulder to cry on. But you're going to get through it. You will. You're so strong. I admire you so much for being able to just pick up the pieces of your shattered life and build something completely new."

Sarah squeezed Ava's hand. "Well, we better get some rest. Tomorrow, we start our grueling 30-hour drive. It's going to be a boring drive through deserts. There's not going to be much to see on the way there. I just want to prepare you. Trust me, the southern route from the Western part of the United States to the east is so boring. I made that trip with our mom. Now we're going in reverse, and it's going to be just as boring. We can always play count the tumbleweeds, but that'll be the only entertainment we'll have on the way out there."

Ava just laughed. "Count the tumbleweeds is a fine game," she said. "I played it before. Another fun game is trying to keep your car on the road when it's super windy outside."

Sarah just raised her eyebrows. "What about the game of trying to not have a tire blowout in the middle of the desert? Actually, that's a better game to play in the middle of summer, when the pavement is so hot that a tire blowout is a real possibility."

"Related to that is counting the number of tire rubbers on the side of the road," Ava said.

Sarah laughed as she thought of a memory she had when she took the train from Monterey to Texas. It was during a period of time when she and Nolan were on the outs, and Sarah was going to Texas to see a friend and didn't have the money to fly. She never had her own money when she was with Nolan, which disgusted her. But an old college buddy friend was going through a bad time with her husband and wanted Sarah to come out and visit. So, her old friend, Joy, sent Sarah money to visit her in Dallas.

Sarah rode the train out to save money. It was a horrible trip. She couldn't sleep on the train because she could never lay down, as somebody was always sitting next to her. It was uncomfortable and cramped.

But there was a funny moment. There came an announcement over the PA system about a couple who was forced off the train at a random station in the middle of the desert. At their expense, they would have to get a different train to get to their destination. Their crime? They smoked in the bathroom, were warned not to do it again, they did it again, and they got booted. The train conductor wanted everyone to know they weren't messing around. No smoking meant no smoking.

A part of Sarah felt a bit sorry for the couple. She'd never been a smoker, but, from what she understood, once a nicotine fit kicked in, things got pretty ugly. She couldn't imagine going for 20 + hours without a cigarette if you were in the active throes of a nicotine addiction. But, at the same time, they were warned. So, there they were, with their bags at a random station in the middle of the desert, having to book another train to get them to where they were going.

Sarah thought it was funny yet sad at the same time. She was relieved she wasn't the one who was getting booted off the train. But she had to have some respect for the train enforcing the rules in such a stringent manner. That conductor wasn't playing, that was for sure.

The next day, Sarah and Ava started their trip out West. Sarah was in contact with Max, who had arrived at Mary's house and was resting comfortably in her spare bedroom. Mary apparently had a small house in Malibu. There were only a couple of spare bedrooms, so Max arranged for Sarah to stay in a hotel on a Malibu beach.

Sarah hung up the phone and looked at Ava. They were still in the hotel room in New Orleans, but the SUV was packed up and ready to roll. "Max is there," Sarah said. "His sister lives in Malibu, so I imagine it's probably a fairly nice place even if it's very small."

"Didn't Max say that Mary couldn't take Julia because Mary didn't have the money to support her?"

"Yeah. Mary is an artist. She was married to a guy who inherited a house in Malibu from his parents, but her husband was also an artist. He was killed in a car accident about five years ago and didn't have life insurance. So, from what I understand, Mary's house is worth over $2 million, which is actually cheap for Malibu, but she really doesn't have a very good income, and her property taxes for that place are through the roof."

Ava just nodded her head. "California real estate, it's crazy. A small house with three bedrooms, and it's over $2 million. If that were me, I'd sell that house, move to some-place like Kansas City, and live like a queen."

"Oh, but I'd imagine the rugged beauty of Malibu would be so inspiring to an artist. I can understand why she'd want to stay in that house. Kansas City is awesome, I'll admit, but there's nothing out there that takes your breath away like the beauty of a place like Malibu. But you're right. She could live like a queen if she moved away to a place with much lower real estate, like the Midwest or even the desert in New Mexico."

The two women got into the SUV and started toward California.

"California, here we come!" Sarah said with a laugh. She started out in California, and now she was going back.

But the reason why she was going back made her very sad.

Chapter Twelve

Willow

There was one problem with Willow's plan to be a ghost writer for the Fitzgerald project - Willow didn't know what she was doing. She'd never written a script before. She'd never written so much as a short story before. She did well in her creative writing classes in college, but her instructors never singled her out for excessive praise.

Willow put her head in her hands as she thought about how she would be able to convince Nancy Tallow that she was the ghost writer she was looking for. "Zelda, the more I think about this Fitzgerald thing, the stupider the entire idea seems," Willow admitted. "I'm going to meet with Nancy, offer my services, she's going to ask for some writing samples and then the jig will be up."

Clara grinned. "Jig will be up," she said. "I like that. What does it mean?"

Willow was surprised that there was an idiom that Clara didn't know. She seemed to know them all. "It means Nancy will know I don't know my ass from a hole in the ground when it comes to screenplay writing, and she'll let the door hit me on the way out."

Willow smiled when she saw that Clara was trying to figure out the other two idioms Willow just threw at her. "Ass from a hole in the ground? Door hitting you on the way out?" she asked.

"What I'm trying to say is that I've never, ever written a screenplay before. I get that Nancy will be looking for a ghost writer for this project, because I'm feeling like she doesn't want it, but she sure won't be looking at me to be that ghost writer. She's going to want an experienced script writer, script doctor or ghost writer. It won't work."

Zelda was looking hopeless again. "So, you're saying that you probably won't be able to do the Fitzgerald screenplay?" she asked.

"Just a second," Clara said, popping her gum. "I'll be right back."

"Where are you going?" Willow asked.

"I'm gonna go to that Nancy dame's house and see if there's anything I can find out that can help you."

In a matter of seconds, Clara was back.

"That was quick," Willow said.

"Yeah, time's different for us if we want it to be," Clara said. "Sometimes, time's the same. Other times, we can be gone for days or months even, and no time at all has passed for you."

"I see," Willow said. She was still getting used to the ghost's rules. "What did you find out?"

"You're in luck, toots," Clara said. "That Nancy broad, she sees a psychic every week. I saw her appointment calendar, and she sees a psychic named Donna."

Willow closed her eyes, finding herself on Nancy's wavelength. She was trying to figure out how trusted Donna's advice was for Nancy.

The messages she received in return were clear - Nancy trusted Donna implicitly. She, indeed, saw Donna every week, and everything Donna told her, Nancy followed to the letter. Nancy even bought different things from Donna, like blessed candles, blessed crystals and blessed herbs.

Willow then concentrated on Donna. Was Donna the real deal, or was she somebody who slapped the word "psychic" over her door and just took people's money for no reason?

Again, the messages from the universe was clear. Donna was a real psychic.

Willow knew what she could do. She could go and see Donna, explain to her that she, Willow, was going to write a screenplay on the Fitzgeralds, with Zelda helping her write the script. She could ask Donna to advise Nancy to hire her for the position as ghost writer.

That was the only thing that would work. The only other thing Willow could possibly do would be to somehow bang out a script that weekend, so she could give Nancy the script when she met with her, and hope for the best. But, considering the fact that Willow didn't even know how to write a script, she couldn't imagine getting an entire screenplay finished in a weekend.

Willow called Donna and made an appointment to see her.

And then she lit some candles, did some meditating and prayed that this would work.

Chapter Thirteen

Willow

Willow met with Donna the next day. She brought Zelda with her and was very encouraged when Donna looked at Willow and then at Zelda and smiled at both of them.

"I take it you're Willow Killeen," Donna said. "And who is this with you?" Donna was looking right at Zelda, her dark eyes dancing. "She looks familiar. She's obviously from the 20s, which was my favorite era. One of my past lives was in the 1920s, and trust me, in that life, I had a ball. Back then, people partied and danced all night long."

"I'm Zelda," Zelda said to Donna.

At that, Donna started clapping her hands together delightedly. "Zelda Fitzgerald? Oh, how exciting for you, Willow, to be visited by such a famous and esteemed woman. I've always been fascinated with the 1920s because, like I said, I had a past life in the 20s. And two women from the 1920s have fascinated me more than any other for various reasons. One is Zelda Fitzgerald, and the other is Coco Chanel."

Zelda could talk to Donna just like she was able to talk to Willow, so Zelda asked the psychic a direct question. "Coco Chanel and me?" Zelda asked. "Coco is a legend. She had such raw talent and could build an empire with her two hands. I'm very flattered to be mentioned in the same breath as Coco because I didn't really accomplish anything in my life."

Donna waved her hand dismissively to Zelda. "Listen, Coco didn't exactly go from French orphan to billionaire fashion designer without help. Don't forget, she had the beauty, charisma, and magnetism to wrap very wealthy men around her little finger. Those wealthy men were the ones who got her started in business. They provided the money for her startups and introduced her to their wealthy female friends, who wore her hats. Because they were wearing her hats, everybody else also wanted her hats. These wealthy women were like today's influencers on Instagram. Without those wealthy men and the women they ran with, Coco would've been a seamstress and probably nothing more."

"So, what are you trying to say?" Zelda asked Donna. "Just because Coco had wealthy men behind her didn't mean she didn't make it on her own."

"Of course not," Donna said. "Coco Chanel had the talent and the vision to make it huge. She also had impec-cable timing because when she came on the scene, women were ready to move out of the corsets into something much more relaxing and freeing. It was such a metaphor for that time, too. Women were coming out of the strictures that society had put on them before. Society was putting them into tight spiritual corsets. Women were being kept down for so long, but by the 1920s, they were experiencing the kind of freedom they'd never had before. The new, less restrictive clothing was just a sign that women were ready to throw off the yoke of oppression. Coco's clothes, emphasizing comfort and style, were perfect for the time."

"That's right," Zelda said, nodding her head. "We were ready to throw off our binds, and we were ready to stop having our inner organs crushed by the corsets that men wanted us to wear. And we were ready to stop having our spirits crushed by the corsets society imposed on our souls. Coco came along and made clothes for that purpose."

"Of course," Donna said. "So Coco definitely had the talent, drive, the business sense, and the timing. I never meant to imply she only made it big because of wealthy men. I'm saying she had help in the beginning, and that was crucial. That's what was missing in your life, Zelda. You never had anybody who wanted to nurture your talents. So don't think you were inferior to Coco Chanel or anybody else. People rarely make it big on their own. They always say that behind every great man is a great woman, and that's true. And behind every great woman was somebody helping her, too. When you don't have that, you can't reach your potential. You didn't have that."

Zelda nodded her head and smiled. "You really understand me," she said to Donna. "And you're making me realize that my failures weren't because I didn't have the talent and the spirit, but because I didn't have the support system. That was a big difference between Coco and me. But other women I admired in my day, like my good friend Tallulah Bankhead and my contemporary, Edna St. Vincent Millay, made it big on their own. Not to mention Clara Bow, the ghost I've been paired up with."

"Well," Donna said. "All those women you just talked about had one thing in common. They didn't get sucked in with toxic men. In fact, Millay and Tallulah were bisexuals. Edna St. Vincent Millay eventually married, but the man she married was a feminist who supported her, nurtured her and did the domestic chores while she made a name. As for Clara, as I'm sure you know, since you and she have been paired up together, she always had complete and total freedom in her life. In other words, the women you admired were not being kept down by anybody. That's really key. So, I guess the moral of the story is, if you want to attain your potential in this world, and you're a woman, you either have to have a support system or you need to have complete and total freedom. You had neither."

Zelda was rapidly nodding her head like she was finally getting it. More than that, she was happy to be validated by this new woman.

Donna sat down. "I'm so happy to see Zelda Fitzgerald in this space. To tell you the truth, I've always wanted to talk to her. Tell her that what happened to her wasn't her fault. However, I feel that's not why you're here, Willow. I'm at a bit of a loss as to exactly what the visit is about. I think you're here on a mission, though. That much I've figured out."

Willow just nodded her head and smiled. "Yep. You figured it out. I knew you would because the universe told me you were the real deal. But you have a regular client whose name is Nancy Tallow. And-"

"Right. Now I understand what you're getting at. What do you need me to do?"

"I'm also a psychic, and I have a good hunch that Nancy is struggling to write the Fitzgerald biopic screenplay. I believe she might start looking for a ghostwriter because she can't complete the project. I'd like you to give her my name and tell her that I'll do a terrific job as a ghostwriter for the project because I have Zelda herself helping me."

Donna nodded her head. "I take it you don't have experience in screenwriting?"

"You got it. I've never written a screenplay in my life. But I must do this because I want Zelda's story told right, and so does she. We both are very interested in making sure this movie tells her story the way she'd want it to be told."

Donna narrowed her eyes and took a deep breath. "Let me throw out some cards and see what comes up," she said. Then she got some tarot cards, shuffled them, and spread them out. She nodded her head.

"I'm sure I don't need to tell you that this spread is very, very positive," she said as she pointed to the tarot spread that was in the form of a Celtic Cross, which was a very common spread that tarot readers used. "What's crossing you is fear, however. You're afraid that Nancy will tell you no, and then you'll be out in the cold. But, as you can see, the Sun card is in your future, the outcome is The Chariot, and The Magician is in your environment."

Willow looked at the tarot spread and saw the spread couldn't be more positive. The Magician in the environment was a very good sign, as The Magician signified that there would be a spark of creativity that would form into a very successful artistic endeavor. The Sun card in the future showed there was going to be nothing but positivity surrounding this project, and The Chariot showed victory was at hand. What was more, since these were all Major Arcana cards that were coming up, the future was set in stone. The Minor Arcana cards, which were the numbered cards, pointed to a future that was in flux, and, while the cards might seem positive or negative, things could change. But anytime the spread showed Major Arcana cards that were extremely positive, it was a sign that things would go extremely well.

"See," Willow said to Donna. "You can be confident when you tell Nancy that I'm going to be the one she's going to want for this project. And I understand that Nancy listens to you and follows your advice."

In that way, Nancy was like another Nancy, Nancy Reagan, who was famous for having an astrologer whom she listened to and whose advice she followed and passed to her husband, Ronald Reagan. That astrologer gave Nancy Reagan certain days that would be good for her husband and days that would not be so good. Nancy followed the advice to the letter.

People thought it was strange that the First Lady would do that, and Willow, of course, didn't find it weird at all. All this happened long before Willow was even born, but she knew the stories, and she thought that Nancy's slings and arrows for this practice were misguided at best. To Willow, everybody should have their own personal astrologer psychic to guide them through life. What was wrong with any of that?

And Nancy Tallow, living in Hollywood and intimately involved in the movie industry, probably wasn't looked down upon for living her life by a psychic's words. She was no doubt not alone in relying on a psychic.

"So, when Nancy Tallow comes to see me to ask me if you should hire you, I should tell her to go for it. I hope you don't mind that I tell her exactly why I think you're going to be amazing on this – you have Zelda herself telling you her story."

"Right. And I hope she comes to ask you about it,"

Willow said. "If she doesn't, she'll probably turn me down flat, and I won't blame her."

Donna nodded her head. "I'll not just tell her that she should hire you. I'll tell her she'll be crazy if she doesn't."

And that was exactly what Willow wanted to hear.

Chapter Fourteen

Sarah

After three long days on the road with Ava, Sarah and Ava finally reached the destination of Malibu, California. As Sarah smelled the California air, which was cool and crisp and slightly salty, and admired the rugged coast as she and Ava drove along the road to Mary's home, Sarah got a pang in her heart. She was homesick. She'd spent over three decades in California, getting her Master's degree at Berkeley, living in Los Angeles for a couple of years before she met Nolan, and then living in Monterey.

She loved The Golden State. She loved how there were so many different terrains and climates in a small area. There were deserts, mountains, and beaches clustered together in certain places. There were miles of rugged coast, where the bluffs hovered one hundred feet or more above the clear blue sea below.

There was so much of a different vibe in California than in Nantucket. California was a golden state settled by people seeking gold in the 1800s. It had since become a haven for surfers, artists, aging hippies, Whole Foods-shopping yuppies, techies and free-spirited wanderers of every stripe. It was where veganism thrived, and animal welfare was taken seriously. Cars in California had to pass emissions standards, so smog was no longer a problem in Los Angeles.

California was a place that seemed to be the very epitome of the live-and-let-live ethos that marked the freedom-loving daydreamers who inhabited the beautiful golden coast.

There were palm trees everywhere. That was one of the many things that Sarah missed when she was on Nantucket. There were all kinds of different palm trees - tall skinny ones that shut up over 100 feet into the air; the fuller and stockier ones with the thick trunks and even thicker fan palms that stuck out of the top in all directions; the short ones that also had very thick fan palms.

And the flowers were so beautiful and in bloom year-round. Sarah's favorite was the Bougainvilleas, the colorful flowers that grew in huge bushes all around California. They were bright pink, red, white, yellow and various colors of purple. The older bougainvillea flowers would grow over 10 feet high in bushes that often covered entire fences. There were the Zinnias and Dahlias, the huge, bright flowers that resembled enormous lollipops and pom-poms. There were the Lantanas, which grew in small shrubs around the area, and sported thousands of small flowers that were typically red and yellow or bright purple.

California was where you could hike up a mountain, then drive a half-hour, end up in the desert in one direction, and on the beach a half-hour in the other direction. For a nature lover and wanderer like Sarah, California was a haven. She loved surfing, hiking, parasailing, kayaking, and climbing rocks. She could do all these things year-round in California, and she missed that. She could do those things in Nantucket, too, although Nantucket didn't have mountains to climb, and she could only do outdoor sports during the warm months. Sarah hated that throughout most of the year, it was too cold in Nantucket to do all the things she enjoyed doing in California.

She breathed the air and felt like she was home.

Ava seemed to sense the difference in her sister. "You really love it out here, don't you?" Ava asked.

Sarah nodded her head. "I do. All things being equal, if I had my sister and good friends out here, I'd much rather live in California than on the East Coast. It suits my vibe so much better than anywhere else I've ever lived. I got my Master's degree in California at Berkeley, got my first job in California in Los Angeles, and lived out here for decades in Monterey. There are wineries up and down the state and world-famous wine areas like Napa and Sonoma. I love it out here."

Ava nodded her head. "I don't have the same roots in California as you, but I understand why you love it out here. You even look like a stereotypical California girl. I've always thought you weren't as happy out in Nantucket as you could be. I know you're happy out there, but only because I'm out there, and you've made such good friends on Nantucket."

"Right," Sarah admitted. "And when I was out here, living in Monterey, I just didn't have anybody who cared about me. I got so sucked into such a plastic way of life when I was out here. I should've gotten involved in the artist communities in Carmel-by-the-Sea. That was a beautiful little town that was only 4 miles away or so from where I lived in Monterey, and that town is such a haven for artists and writers and poets and just the kind of people that I should've been associating myself with."

Sarah looked a little bit sad.

"Yeah," Ava said. "If you would've befriended artists and writers instead of becoming friends with wealthy women of leisure, I doubt you would've gotten involved with a cocaine charge you had nothing to do with. To say the very least."

Sarah just laughed. "You might say that. But I had a certain image when I lived out here. It was an image culti-vated for me by Nolan, not myself, and that image had to be upheld. We spent weekends on Nolan's yacht, hanging around the most plastic people you'd ever want to meet. I didn't think artists, writers, and poets would be interested in hanging around on yachts, so I associated myself with people who liked that type of thing. And it was all such a downfall, running away from who I really was."

Sarah and Ava found a lookout spot on a bluff, and they both had a pair of binoculars, so they could see a colony of sea lions just down below. It wasn't quite pupping season, as the pups were usually born between May and June, but there were quite a few adults down on the rocks below. The male sea lions were huge, sometimes twice as big as the females, and their voices were quite loud. The males were the ones who had the distinctive bark that people associated with the mammal. The females were quite a bit smaller and didn't bark so much as growl.

Down below, the sea lions were sleeping on the rocks, but a few males were standing guard and barking their heads off.

Sarah was always so entertained by these animals. Growing up in Kansas City, where she could only see sea lions in the zoo, she enjoyed watching the animals swimming around in their pool. It was the sea lions and the hippos that always attracted young Sarah in the Kansas City Zoo. Even now, whenever she saw the sea lions in the wild lying around on the rocks, she was so fascinated by them that she could watch them for hours.

Ava smiled as she watched the sea lions through her binoculars. "Tell me a little about these guys," Ava said to Sarah.

"What do you want to know?" Sarah asked.

"Just anything you want to tell me. Watching them is a lot of fun, so I'm naturally curious about them."

"Well, right now, it's neither mating nor pupping season," Sarah said. "They mate from June to August, and the pups are born between May and June, so we're just a little bit early to see the new pups. But watching them when the pups are around is a lot of fun. They live in colonies that can have thousands of members. The members of the colonies all swim together and hang out together on the rocks. One male has a harem of around 30 females that he mates with. So it's like a pride of lions, with the male at the top of the hierarchy, and a harem of females below him, only instead of the pride living isolated from other prides, there are a whole bunch of prides living together."

Ava put her binoculars down and looked at Sarah. "Fascinating," she said. "How do you know so much about these animals?"

"I read a lot about them because I love watching them so much. And I've also talked to some guys from the Sierra Club. These guys like to go and talk to tourists who are watching the animals because they need to make sure that people respect them as the wild animals they are. They look so cute and cuddly, and people want to go right up to them, but they're very territorial, they're predators, and they'll attack anybody who gets too close to them."

Ava raised her binoculars again and smiled. "Wait, didn't I read about some people being chased off by angry sea lions in San Diego?"

"It was in La Jolla, a small city just north of San Diego. And yes, there was a funny video of some sea lions chasing after some people. But I've been down there, watching the people who snorkel in that area and sea lions coexist with them. The sea lions swim alongside the snorkelers. Those sea lions that chased the beachgoers that day were females, and they were probably protecting their young."

Ava laughed. "I remember seeing that video. It was hilarious watching those animals waddling after the people. But I'm sure the sea lions didn't exactly find it hilarious that the people were encroaching on their space."

Sarah just breathed in the air some more. "Seeing these animals is another thing I really miss. We obviously don't see them in Nantucket. But out here in California, they just run wild and free. Sea lions, and pelicans, these are just a couple of things that we don't see on Nantucket. You don't get these beautiful tropical plants out there, either."

Ava squinted at her sister. "You ever think about moving out here again?"

Sarah never thought about it, but only because she'd put it out of her mind. And now, with Julia coming to live with her, her moving back to California was out of the question. So, it just wasn't something she wanted to think about.

"No. I don't even think about it. I've made my life on Nantucket. I have you guys out there, and I'll soon have Julia living with me. Julia will need stability in her life more than anything else right now. So, I just can't uproot her. I've made a promise to Max that I was going to make her life as stress-free as possible. She's made many friends in her school, she really likes it on Nantucket, and that's where she belongs."

Ava nodded her head. "Sarah, I hate to say it, but it sounds like you're still living for other people. Don't forget, Julia's aunt lives out here. There's a possibility that maybe Julia wants to be out here if she and her aunt are close. Her aunt is connected to her father, which is pretty powerful."

The two women walked along a trail where they could see the vast expanse of the Pacific Ocean right below them. Sarah was thinking about Ava's words. Ava was making a certain amount of sense, like she always did. What if Julia wanted to live in California to be close to her aunt? Julia was adamant that she wanted to stay on Nantucket, but she would stay with her aunt for the next few months. There was a possibility that Julia would get attached to her aunt while she was out here. Her aunt couldn't take Julia on because Max said Mary wasn't financially secure enough to raise a child. So Sarah wasn't necessarily fearing that Julia would want to stay with Mary instead of her.

But what if Julia wanted to stay close to Mary? Would Sarah be willing to move to California so Julia could stay close to her aunt? Sarah had to admit her interest in wine, and her certification as a sommelier, were much more suited to California than Nantucket. Nantucket had no vineyards because the climate wasn't suitable for growing grapes.

On the other hand, California, in general, was known for its wines. And the vineyards and the wineries weren't just concentrated in areas like Napa, Sonoma, and Temecula, but even the Los Angeles area had some vineyards and wineries, including several right there in Malibu. Sarah could seamlessly find a job at any number of wineries in the area and could even buy a winery of her own if she moved out to California.

She would miss her support system, that was for sure. Her sister, her new best friends, Hallie and Quinn, and Emerson had all managed to burrow right into her heart.

Ava walked alongside Sarah, swinging her arms and looking out onto the ocean. "See, I'm asking you these questions because Quinn is moving out here to Los Angeles for Emerson. As you know, Emerson is enrolled in the middle school there on Nantucket, and she's just not challenged enough in her classes. But, more than that, Emerson wants to attend a performing arts school. You know she's a violin virtuoso, and Quinn has been looking at some schools out here in Los Angeles that would be able to nurture her talent. She also has looked in New York City, but it seems that Los Angeles is the front-runner right now."

This was the first Sarah heard that maybe Quinn was looking to leave Nantucket. "Wow. She would do that for her daughter?"

"Quinn would do anything for Emerson, and that's the God's honest truth. Quinn was trying to talk me into coming out here to Los Angeles because she thinks I should be closer to Jackson. And Samantha really wants to move out here because her boyfriend published his novel, it's been tearing up the charts, and he's been getting interest from Hollywood. Samantha feels that while she's doing quite well on Nantucket with her cake decorating thing, she could break out in Los Angeles with all the wealthy people who hold events and weddings. She's actually had a headhunter from one of the largest caterers in L.A. try to recruit her, and she's seriously thinking about jumping at the chance. Plus, she wants to be closer to her brother, who she has always been close to."

"So, you would move out here?" Sarah asked.

"I would," Ava said. "To be closer to Jackson and Samantha, as well as staying close to Quinn and Emerson."

"And what about Hallie?" Sarah said. "We can't just leave her all alone on Nantucket. That place is so insular and quiet most of the year. I can't imagine she'd be thrilled to be abandoned by her friends to fend for herself."

Ava just laughed. "Are you kidding me? Los Angeles is ground zero for alternative healing spas, and she wants to get her life coaching business off the ground. She would have much more opportunity here to do all of that."

Sarah was starting to really like the sound of all of this. "When can you sell that house on Nantucket? I thought you had to wait five years, or else you'd forfeit it."

"Jessica's been doing a fantastic job of running it. Then again, she might end up out here, too, because James needs to be closer to the recording industry. He's out on Nantucket because he's madly in love with Jessica, and I think she's in love with him too. I wouldn't be surprised if they tied the knot and moved out here. So, I don't know, I'd have to figure out if there was a loophole in the will that I could drive a truck through it and sell the place early."

"Could you just hire somebody to manage the place, and you could move out here and buy a house or something?" Sarah asked. "After all, Christopher gave the money back he stole, and you made a lot of money off your bed-and-breakfast last summer, money I'm sure you squirreled away. You have a lot of experience running a bed-and-breakfast, so you could come to work out here at a bed and breakfast or manage a resort of some sort."

The two ladies stopped and took in the view for a few moments. "I had planned to stay put right where I am, but I have to admit that if you moved back here, Samantha moved out here for Grayson, and Quinn came out here for Emerson, I'd be sorely tempted to come out here as well," Ava said. "I'd love to be closer to Jackson. If both Samantha and Jackson were living out here, and my sister and best friend were also here, I think I'd have to follow everybody out here. You're right. I could hire somebody to run my place until I can sell it. But I'd like to see a lawyer to see if I could sell early. I'd love to have the money from selling the place on Nantucket to have out here in California because it's so expensive to live out here."

"It's expensive to live out here because it's so desirable to live out here," Sarah said. "The weather can't be beat. Just think, we'd never have to worry about a hurricane again, and we'd never have to worry about shoveling snow. The water out here is so clear and blue, the vibe is so distinctive, and it's a vibe that definitely fits more with my basic nature than Nantucket ever did. I miss going out to the desert, camping amongst the Joshua trees, and dune buggying through all the sand dunes."

Sarah was starting to warm to the idea of the entire clan moving out to California, but she didn't want to get ahead of herself. She had to consider Julia's feelings. If the young girl was adamant about staying on Nantucket, that's what Sarah would do.

Ava was right. Sarah was living for other people, namely Max and Julia, but that was what responsible adults did. They make a commitment, and they stick to it, their own feelings being subverted to the needs and wants of some-body else. That was a recipe for unhappiness, of course – Sarah had just spent the last 20 plus years of her life living for somebody else.

She felt she'd gotten away from that and found herself on Nantucket, but did she really? Or did she just tell herself that she was happy there on Nantucket, where she didn't really have much to do for most of the year because she was a sommelier for Ava, and Ava's business was dead through most of the year? Was she still trying to fit a square peg into a round hole? There was no doubt that her wine skills would be much more in demand in California, in the middle of wine country, and there would be no downtime for her and her skills.

The way she was feeling out here, like she belonged here, made her realize that she was just telling herself a lie this past year or so. She had tried to convince herself that Nantucket was where she belonged because she was afraid of being alone, and she'd found such a community on Nantucket. She tried to ignore the inner nagging feeling that she was wasting her time out on Nantucket Island, not to mention her talents.

By now, the sun was setting, and a brilliant orange filled the sky over the water. "You know, there was always a legend about the sunsets here in California. Supposedly, on rare occasions, you could see a flash of green right when the sun hits the water. But I've never known anybody who saw the flash of green, so I still think it's just a legend."

Maybe the green flash was a legend, but what certainly wasn't a legend was that the sunsets over the Pacific Ocean were absolutely gorgeous. Sarah was always astounded about how quickly the sun would disappear below the water. It would seem that the sun would be just above the water, then, not more than a few minutes later, it would disappear, leaving darkness behind.

The two ladies got into the SUV and headed to Sarah's hotel room in the Malibu Beach Inn, located right on the beach. Their room was all luxury, with a beachfront terrace, a fireplace in the room and a view of the ocean. Max had booked the place for Sarah because he knew Sarah wouldn't be able to stay with his sister. Sarah was happy about staying in the hotel because she didn't want to be in the way.

That evening, Ava and Sarah sat on the terrace, drank wine, and listened to the ocean coming in. It was much like what they did in Nantucket when they always hung out on Ava's rooftop terrace. Yet, it was also different somehow. It wasn't just that palm trees and beautiful flowers were surrounding the property. It wasn't that there were scores of little tiny lizards scampering about the patio. It wasn't that the air was warm, or at least it was much warmer than it was on Nantucket.

No, it felt different because Sarah finally felt that she was home.

Chapter Fifteen

Willow

Willow met with Nancy the very next day. Caffee Luxxe was a Santa Monica Café where it was fashionable for people to work on screenplays, meet critique groups, and talk to others who were in the same boat. Above all, it was a good place to make contacts.

Nancy stood and shook Willow's hand when Willow came in the door. She had her laptop in front of her and a large coffee she was working on. It apparently was her third coffee in the morning, as there were two other paper cups on the table.

Willow sat down when Nancy invited her to. Nancy seemed to be very glad to see her. "I have to admit, I'm so excited to talk to you. I've been overwhelmed with working on a screenplay for a major movie that's going to be produced in the fall, and I got this Scott Fitzgerald project dumped in my lap by my agent. I'm sorry. I just can't bring myself to care about the subject. I'm not generally a historical fiction type of gal. I prefer to work on action movies and superhero films. I have no idea why I was tapped to write this screenplay, and I've been looking for a ghostwriter for it. It seems like you calling me was like fate or something."

The barista called Willow's name, and she went up and got her coffee, which was apparently ready. Willow sat back down and took a sip of her coffee. She decided she would just have to put her cards on the table to see if Nancy bit. "I'd like to go ahead and be a ghostwriter for this project, but I have to be honest with you. I'm not a screenwriter. In fact, I've never written anything in my life."

Nancy looked at Willow with dismay. "I don't understand. When you called me, I assumed you were an experienced screenwriter, as ghostwriters typically are. Why are you wasting my time?"

"Listen, I'm going to tell you something, and I'd like you to run what I'm telling you by a psychic. But I'm very anxious to be a ghostwriter for your project because I'm a psychic and sometimes in touch with the spiritual world. And I've recently been in touch with Zelda Fitzgerald. In fact, she's in this coffee house right now."

That was true, as Zelda was standing right behind another guy working on a screenplay. Zelda had admitted to Willow that she was unfamiliar with writing screenplays, so she wanted to watch a screenwriter at work while Willow talked to Nancy. Zelda was very intent on watching the guy work on his project, so intent that she wasn't even looking in Willow's direction.

Clara was nowhere to be found. She'd told Willow that morning that she was going to explore the city a bit. "I'm curious about how much things have changed since I lived here," Clara had explained about why she was going to look around Los Angeles instead of going to the coffee house with Willow and Zelda. Zelda was more than happy to be rid of Clara for the day because Zelda didn't think Clara would bring anything beneficial to the meeting, and she'd just be in the way. Willow had to admit that that was probably true.

Nancy looked at Willow with a curious look, but she certainly didn't look hostile to the idea that there was a ghost around that was going to help Willow with writing the screenplay. Most people would've looked at Willow like she had grown a second head right there in the coffeehouse and would've stormed off. But Nancy just furrowed her brow a little bit.

"Just a second," she said. "I think I need another coffee before I talk to you about this. I'll be right back."

Willow imagined that maybe Nancy would go up to the barista and pretend to order a coffee when she actually was calling the loony bin to report her. But Nancy just got another coffee and sat back down.

"Now, what were you saying? You're being haunted by Zelda Fitzgerald, and she's in this coffeehouse right now?"

"Right. That's exactly what I just told you. And that's the reason why I want to do this screenplay, and that's why I know I can do a good job with it."

Nancy nodded her head and took a sip of her coffee. "How do I know what you're saying is true? I'll be honest, I'm tempted to tell you to turn right around, leave the coffee house and never bug me again. You have to tell me why I'm not going to end up doing that."

Willow cleared her throat. "Talk to Donna about it," she said. "She'll tell you everything you need to know."

Nancy bit her bottom lip, took another sip of her coffee, and seemed to contemplate what Willow was telling her.

"Well, the cat's already out of the bag about how much I listen to Donna for my career advice. I'm sure you understand, because you're also a psychic. All I know is I've been in this town for 10 years, and she's never steered me wrong, ever. I mean, look at me. I'm a working screenwriter. A female working screenwriter, at that. That didn't just happen by accident. Every time I have a project, I go to Donna for advice. So, I'm not shy to tell you that I'm going to do that with this, as well."

Willow nodded her head, liking the sound of what Nancy was saying. If she listened to Donna, then she was going to be in.

"Go for it, dude," Willow said. "Talk to Donna, then get back with me."

Nancy nodded her head. "What's it like, being in touch with the spirit world? Is it weird?"

Willow didn't want to be honest about that. Truth be told, before Zelda and Clara showed up, it had been a long time since since she had been visited by a spirit or a ghost. And it had been a really long time since Willow was visited by a ghost who wanted her to do something specific for that ghost. Willow hated being manipulated by anybody. She never wanted to give up control of her life, and that's exactly what the ghosts were doing to her – they were taking away her control. In the process, they were altering her life, because she wasn't able to be at her spa day, giving her regular clients their treatments.

Willow was understandably angry that there was a possibility that her regular clients would just find somebody else while she was gone. They might never come back. All because she had two pushy ghosts who didn't know how to take the word "no" for an answer.

"To tell you the truth, it sucks. Ghosts and spirits have

the means to make your life a living hell if they want to. Trust me, I'd rather be anywhere but here in Los Angeles. But, here I am, getting stuck with writing a screenplay. God knows how long I'm going to be out here. In the meantime, I have an alternative healing spa on Nantucket that I'm neglecting. I don't even know if I'm going to have a business when I go back."

Then Willow bowed her head and spoke in a low voice, lest Zelda might hear her. At the moment, Zelda was still, thankfully, engrossed in watching this screenwriting guy across the room work away on his computer. "And Zelda is very pushy. So is Clara Bow, but I get along with her a lot more than I do Zelda, because Clara Bow is a sweety."

Nancy's eyes got wide. "You're being haunted by Clara Bow too? I love her. I've seen all of her movies, and she made quite a few of them, and nobody has commanded a screen like her, before or since. You just can't take your eyes off her when she's on screen. They didn't call her the 'It Girl' for no reason, you know."

"Yeah, and, to tell you the truth, I'm kinda warming up to her," Willow said. "She's not as pushy as Zelda. She was like that in life, too. Just a sweet, good-natured girl who happened to make it huge on the big screen. Zelda, in her life, was much more complicated, to say the very least. And, it's not surprising that in their afterlife, they retain much of their essence. So, that's why I'm here – Zelda is adamant that her story is going to be told in her way."

Nancy nodded her head, and took another sip of coffee. "But this biopic is on Scott, not her. True, he was absolutely obsessed with her from the moment he met her, for what-ever reason, and she was a big part of his life. But there were other aspects of his life that didn't feature her. Don't forget, towards the end of his life, he was involved with somebody else while Zelda was in a mental hospital. I really wasn't going to feature her as prominently as others have. I really wanted to focus on who he was as a person, and why he self-destructed so much."

Willow knew what Nancy was saying was true – there were many aspects about Scott that had nothing to do with his wife. It sounded like Nancy was going to take the biopic in the direction that deemphasized Zelda's role in the marriage.

Willow knew Zelda wouldn't be happy with the direction the project was taking. From what Willow knew about the woman, Zelda would take it as a slight if a movie came out about Scott where she was just a supporting character. A movie like that would be akin to *Walk The Line*, the biopic on Johnny Cash where his wife, June Carter Cash, was a side character and nothing more. Or, more recently, the movie *Elvis*, where Priscilla Presley was hardly shown.

No, Zelda was definitely going to want a starring role in this picture. Willow could certainly write the script to where Zelda was the main character, and Scott was the supporting character, much like the Amazon Prime series treated the couple. That series was definitely told through her eyes, not his, and she was definitely the main character. But Willow knew that if she wrote the script that way, Nancy would be pissed, and rightly so.

That was going to have to be another angle Willow was going to have to figure out.

In the meantime, she was going to have to give Zelda the news that Nancy was looking for a script that deemphasized her role. She wasn't looking forward to having that conversation with the very persnickety ghost.

Willow met with Nancy for the better part of the afternoon. She got Nancy's treatment for the screenplay, and the outline she was going to be working with, and she looked at the treatment and the outline with dismay. *Zelda is not going to like this*, Willow thought. Zelda's character was hardly in either the treatment or the outline. A screenplay treatment was basically a summary of the story line for the movie, and Nancy's treatment was much more of a psychological profile of the writer himself, as opposed to examining Scott's marriage. The treatment that Willow was given focused on Scott's rise and fall, Scott's early days in Princeton, Scott's friendship with Ernest Hemingway (who was no fan of Zelda's), and how Scott's fiction reflected the overall mood of the country.

When Willow finally got a chance to talk to Zelda to break the news to her that her character was going to be, at best, supporting, Zelda took it much differently than Willow anticipated she would. She was very calm, and simply said "we'll see about that."

And then she disappeared.

Clara was around, and she explained to Willow what Zelda was doing. "Ya know, there's one thing this lousy town understands, and that's green. Clams. Kale. Cabbage. Money. Zelda, she's no dumb Dora. She learned a lot today by watching that guy today working on that screenplay. He was also looking on that screen, what do you call it?"

"A computer."

"Yeah. A computer. That guy, he was looking at that computer, and Zelda found out who really has the power in this town. Besides the producers and directors, I mean. But if there's one thing Zelda knows, and I know, if you get a well-known tomato interested in a film, the film's gonna get made. When I was making movies, and they just mentioned my name for a movie, that movie was made."

"Okay. So, what are you trying to say?"

"Zelda, she's visiting somebody tonight. She learned from that guy with that, what do you call it again?"

"A computer," Willow said.

"Yeah, that guy with the computer, I guess he was looking at something about a hot actress named Ellen Ross, who's white-hot right now. Guess she just won an Oscar, and all her movies have gone to number one. Guess Ellen's looking for a new role. Zelda's going to tell this Ellen dame that she needs to take the role of Zelda Fitzgerald in this new movie. I can guarantee that if that Ellen gets involved, suddenly, this movie ain't gonna be about Scott no more. It's gonna be Zelda all the way."

That Zelda was a wily one, Willow thought.

"I assume this Ellen person isn't sensitive," Willow said.

"Right. Thick as a bowling ball, that one. But Zelda's gonna come to her in a dream. That's what we do with people who can't really see us or talk to us. We wait 'til they're sleepin', then we get on in there and tell them what we need them to know. They wake up, tell people about the weirdest dream they had the night before, and they have no idea why they had that dream. Zelda can get the job done, trust me on this. That dame knows how to get what she wants, that's for sure."

The very next day, Willow found out just how right Clara was.

There was a notification on Willow's phone that Ellen Ross was campaigning for the role of Zelda Fitzgerald in the new biopic, and that the movie was going to now focus on Zelda, and not Scott.

Damn, that was fast.

Chapter Sixteen

Sarah

After Sarah and Ava had settled into Sarah's hotel room in Malibu, Max invited her to dinner with Mary, him, and Julia. Max told Sarah that he had some news about Julia, and Sarah braced herself for what that news was going to be. Ava was also invited to come along to the dinner, but she begged off.

"I would just be in the way," Ava said. "But thanks for the invitation. Tonight, I think I might just walk along the beach, and I'm going to call my son and tell him I'm in town. I know he's stressed out about an audition on Tuesday, so I doubt he'll want to see me until after the audition is over."

Sarah knew Ava understood the situation. She didn't want to say as much, but Sarah also thought Ava probably would just be in the way during the dinner. She was grateful her sister was such an understanding sort.

Sarah went over to the small house that was on a cliff

overlooking the beach below. The house was built in the 1920s and had been renovated many times. It was a beautiful concept, with floor-to-ceiling windows that looked out on a back patio, a fireplace, and hardwood floors throughout. Sarah's architectural eye saw a lot of Frank Lloyd Wright's influence in the modernist design.

Mary was a very kind host, giving Sarah a huge hug when she walked in the door. "Sarah, come in, come in," Mary said. She was dressed in a man's work shirt, jeans that hit mid-calf, and her feet were bare. All over the house were paintings on the floor, some hidden behind drop cloths, others were not. The paintings were quite good, very colorful and reflected the natural surroundings. Cliffs, flowers, and sunsets were the backdrop for the human characters in her paintings.

Sarah had a bottle of wine in her hands, and Mary took the bottle of wine from her. "Max tells me you're quite the wine expert," Mary said as she took the bottle of Malbec Sarah had in her hands. "And you've been to Napa and Sonoma quite a few times."

"Yes. When I lived in Monterey, I visited wineries up north just about every weekend. Sonoma and Napa Valley were just day trips for me when I lived in Monterey, so I spent a great deal of time at wineries in those two areas," Sarah said.

Mary nodded her head. "I can tell," she said. "This bottle of wine seems perfect for what I'm serving tonight. I have salmon steaks on the grill, a baked potato, and a nice light salad. I love Malbec with salmon."

Sarah followed Mary onto the patio, where there was a small table and chairs. She saw Julia sitting at the table, but not Max. That worried Sarah. She wondered if Max was resting in his room.

"Max wasn't feeling too well, just out of the blue. I think the trip took a lot out of him because he's been sleeping a lot since he's gotten here." Then she shook her head. "I've really been worried about him. I was hoping I would get a few months, but he had a seizure today. It really gave me a scare." Then she paused. "I don't want to say anything to Julia, but I'm starting to think Max won't have to use the doctor to help him pass on. It'll take a long time to get residency here in California, and I wonder if he'll have that time."

Sarah knew what Mary was talking about. She thought the same thing about Max while driving to the West Coast. He really seemed to be weaker than Sarah had anticipated he would be. And the fact he had a seizure wasn't a good sign at all.

Sarah fought back tears as she felt a lump forming in her throat. Julia looked so small and so sad. Down below, the ocean was raging. It seemed there was a storm at sea, judging by the size of the waves. Julia was sitting at the table in a hoodie pulled up over her head. So far, she hadn't acknowledged Sarah's presence.

Sarah went out to the table and sat next to Julia. Julia barely turned her head when Sarah sat down.

"Dad isn't doing so good," she finally said to Sarah as the two sat and watched the waves come in. "Sarah, I need to talk to you about a few things."

Sarah quietly waited for her to speak. She had a feeling she knew what Julia was about to say.

"I want to stay here. I really don't have a family, except for Mary and my aunt Hannah, although I don't think my aunt Hannah really counts."

Sarah wasn't really prepared to hear that. After all, Max said Mary didn't have the money to care for Julia. "Okay,"

Sarah said. She felt slightly disappointed because she was looking forward to raising the young girl. But, at the same time, Julia's best interest had to be paramount in this situation. If Julia felt she should stay with her aunt Mary, that was what would happen.

"Okay."

Then Julia shook her head. "I want to stay here, but Mary doesn't have the money to watch me. But I really want to stay close to her. I'd forgotten how much I really love her. I hadn't seen her in a long time, but when I saw her, and we spent the past couple of days just talking into the night, I knew I wanted to stay around here."

So, there it was. What Sarah and Ava were talking about was coming to reality. She wondered if Ava was serious about moving out to the West Coast if Sarah and Quinn ended up out here. She also wondered if Quinn was serious about moving out here for her daughter. Moving out to California for Emerson would make a lot of sense. Los Angeles had several performing arts high schools. Emerson would do much better in a performing arts high school than where she was at the moment, a small school that really didn't have a performing arts department to speak of.

Emerson's talent needed to be nurtured, so Sarah knew Quinn probably would end up in Los Angeles. Quinn could also end up back in New York because New York City had plenty of performing arts schools. But Sarah didn't think Quinn would want to go with that option. Quinn hated New York City when she lived there, mainly because she didn't like having to take public transportation everywhere, plus she hated the dirtiness and the grime and how crowded it was. Los Angeles wasn't exactly a clean city, but there were places in that city where you could have a bit of space and a house, and you could definitely have a car in Los

Angeles and get around. That wasn't the case in New York City.

"Julia, are you sure you want to stay out here?" Sarah asked.

Julia nodded her head. "My dad always told me how important family is. He never got along with his sister Hannah, but he always loved Mary. And I really want to stay close to her. I hate to do this to you. I know how much you love Nantucket. And I don't know what will happen if you tell me you don't want to move out here. I'm sorry, Sarah, I really like you. But we don't really know each other all that well. I might have to talk to my dad about making another arrangement. I don't want to go into the system, but that might be what has to happen."

Sarah put her arm around Julia. "Kid, here's the thing. I gave your father my word that I'd make sure you're protected after he passes on. And I don't want you to think I'd move out here against my will just so I can make you happy. On the contrary, I was actually thinking before I came to visit Mary's home how much I missed living in California. How much happier I would be out here than on Nantucket. I'm relieved you want to stay out here because I was afraid your heart was set on staying on Nantucket, and, to tell you the truth, I realized when I got out here that I was ready to move on from that place."

Julia looked at Sarah suspiciously. "You're just saying that. I don't want you to move out here just for me. I can't ask you to do that. I really will be okay if I have to find a foster family. I'll be 18 in five years, and hopefully, I'll go to college. So whatever family gets me, they won't have to put up with me for long."

Sarah bit her bottom lip. "Julia. I spent over 30 years in California. I never wanted to leave. In fact, if I had my way,

I would've still been living in Los Angeles and working for an architectural firm. I loved it there. And I loved living in Monterey."

Sarah didn't want to tell Julia that while she loved Monterey, she didn't love the man she was living with. Julia didn't really need to know how toxic Sarah's relationship was with her ex. That wasn't the young girl's business.

"Why did you come out to Nantucket?" Julia asked.

Sarah took a deep breath. "I was like you, in a way. I was looking to reconnect with my family. I was at a point where I didn't know what to do. I was alone, afraid, shattered. And there was only one person I wanted to be around - my sister, whom I hadn't talked to for over 20 years. Ava took me in at the lowest point in my life, and I'll never forget that. But a lot of things have changed since that time. I sold a very valuable penny for almost $3 million. I got my sommelier's certificate, so I could get a job at a winery very easily. I'm back on my feet, so I don't need Nantucket. And, because Nantucket is such a sleepy little town for so much of the year, there's not much for me to do there. Out here in California, there would be so much more opportunity for me, year-round."

Julia nodded her head. "Are you sure? I mean, it wouldn't be just for me if you came to live out here?"

"No. I'm relieved you want to live out here. I don't know, but I think Emerson might be coming out here, too. Quinn wants more opportunities for her than she can have on Nantucket. I don't think Quinn will want to live in Malibu. She'll probably live closer to Los Angeles because the performing arts high school is in Los Angeles proper. But they'll be living out here if all goes according to plan. So you'll have your best friend out here, too."

Julia's face lit up. "Sarah, I can't believe it's going to

work out. Maybe. I was so afraid to say anything to you. I knew I wanted to stay out here, but I thought you were on Nantucket to stay since you just bought a home there."

Mary came out and brought the salad for everybody to munch on. It was a beautiful salad with greens, pine nuts, Parmesan cheese, tomatoes, radishes, carrots, and cucumbers.

"I just talked to Max, and he's going to try to make it down for dinner," Mary said. "I don't think he's going to want to eat. He hasn't really eaten much since he's gotten here. But he said he would come down here and try to socialize with everybody."

"Then we'll just wait for Max to come down," Sarah said.

Max came down for dinner a few minutes later. He gave Sarah a kiss on the cheek. "Did Julia drop her bomb?" Max asked. "Teenagers. The only thing you can count on with teenagers is that you can't count on them at all. I didn't think Julia would get out here and try to mess everything up."

Sarah took a sip of her wine. "Yeah, we talked. And ironically, Ava and I talked before Julia and I ever did. Before I came to Mary's house, I told Ava I wanted to stay in California because it's my home. It's much more my home than Nantucket ever has been or will be."

Max, like Julia before him, looked suspicious when Sarah told him this. "Listen, I told Julia that she's going to have to put her desires aside if you weren't willing to move out here. It's a lot to ask you to do it. Don't feel obligated. And don't let her guilt you into it, either. I'm sure she probably told you that if you didn't want to move out to California, she'd go into the system. I have news for you, and I have news for Julia – she doesn't get to make that decision.

A court would make that decision, and no court would decide a child should be in foster care if there's a guardian who's more than willing to take custody of the child. So don't let her blackmail you into it."

Sarah closed her eyes. "Max, you're not listening to me. I'm relieved Julia wants to move out here, because I do too. Once I got out here, and I smelled the air and went along the coastline and saw the cliffs, the trees, the flowers, the sea lions on the beach, and the sun set over the water, I really had a pang in my heart. I felt this was where I belonged, but I was willing to stay in Nantucket if Julia wanted to stay there. So when she told me she wanted to move out here, she played my song. I can't tell you how happy it makes me to know I can come back home."

Max started to laugh. "Sounds like things actually worked out the way they were supposed to. I didn't think that was possible in this situation. I thought for sure you and Julia would be at odds."

"Surprise," Sarah said. "We're definitely on the same page."

Max's smile got even bigger. "So you really want to move out here to the West Coast? You know you don't have to find a home in Malibu. But it would be nice if you were willing to live in the Los Angeles area. I know Los Angeles isn't exactly the clean area that Nantucket is. There are a lot of seedy areas of town and a lot of traffic you have to contend with. It'll be quite a shock for you to live here after living in a sleepy place like Nantucket."

"Max, I lived out here for 30 years. Nantucket was a shock to my system after living in California for so long. I really kinda hated it out there. I was running for school board just because I desperately wanted something to do.

And I wanted to make sure that the censorship thing didn't go through. But mainly, I was extremely bored."

Max started to laugh again. "You mean you're not a true believer? You didn't feel you were meant for the school board position on Nantucket? You mean, you used me?" Max was teasing, of course, as was evident from his playful tone.

Sarah laughed, too. "No, I'm a true believer in what I was campaigning on. But it's also a fact that I was just damn bored. And now Emerson will be out here, along with Quinn. At least it looks that way. And I think Ava might end up out here, and if she does, Hallie might too. It would be the best of all possible worlds if I come out here and have my ladies out here as well."

"Perfect," Max said. "I think things just might work out."

Sarah gripped his hand. "Yes, I think things are working out just like they're supposed to."

He kissed her on the forehead. "I'm really crazy about you, you know. I never thought I'd meet a woman like you. You're going to take my daughter in, and you hardly even know her. There are not many women who would do that. You're very special."

Sarah smiled. "You're not so bad, yourself. And I know your daughter got many of your traits, so I'm not worried about having major issues with her. I think you raised her right, so I'm looking forward to raising her the rest of the way."

Mary was watching the two of them with a big smile. "I'm so happy I'm going to have my niece around. She's been a real joy. I can't tell you how much it means to me that I'll be able to see her become an adult. And I just can't wait to see what kind of an adult she becomes. I think she's going to really have a good life. She has all of Max's best traits. His empathy. His sensitivity. His intelligence. His wit. She'll be like a female version of my brother, and that's the highest compliment I can pay."

Behind Mary's smile, there was a distinct sense of sadness. Of course, they all were living under the Sword of Damocles. None of them could be truly happy because Max had little time left.

But, on that day, they were together. They were going to have to make the most of every good day.

And, so far, this was a very good day.

Chapter Seventeen

Willow

Zelda got her way. The biggest female star in the world, Ellen Ross, would star in the Zelda Fitzgerald biopic. And that's what was official – it was going to be Zelda's biopic, not Scott's. As soon as Ellen announced that that would be her project, the producers and the director of the movie decided to take the movie in the direction towards Zelda and away from Scott.

Willow was going to have to meet with Nancy again. As it was, Nancy called Willow that Sunday morning. "Willow, I need to tell you something about the project," Nancy said over the phone.

"I know. It's back to the drawing board for the treatment and the outline."

"You might say that," Nancy said. "I hate it when things like this happen. You do all this work on a screenplay treatment and outline, and boom, people change their minds, and it's off to the races. Drives me absolutely batty. But one good thing about Ellen being on board – this project probably won't go into development hell, and it'll probably be made on an expedited schedule."

"Development hell" was when a project gets stalled for one reason or another. Often, a certain property might be in the hands of one director and producer, with certain stars attached. And then something happens, and it doesn't get made for whatever reason. Sometimes a studio will buy the rights to a book, and they'll get everybody lined up, but if it doesn't go into production within a certain period of time, the rights to the book lapse and everybody starts over again.

Willow had heard about stories where the movie took a decade or more to get made. Along the way, different stars, directors, and studios get involved. Usually, by the time the movie actually does get made, the movie's not very good, and it becomes a box office bomb everybody wants to forget about.

But when an A-list actress or actor, especially one like Ellen, who was *the* top A-list actress at the moment, gets involved, suddenly projects are not in development hell. On the contrary, they often get fast-tracked when there's a superstar attached.

"I assume you'll do a new treatment and outline?" Willow asked.

"Yeah. Unless you want to do it. I'll pay you, of course."

Willow agreed to a flat fee of $5000 for the project. She was obviously going to have to ask for more if she was expected to do the treatment and outline as well.

"You better do it," Willow said. "After all, you're going to be the one who's going to be taking the meeting with the director. The director will tell you what he expects from you now. Since you'll get that information, you'll do better with the treatment and outline."

Nancy sighed. "I was afraid you'd say that," she said. "You're right, of course. It's just that I have such a busy schedule. I didn't want to go back to the drawing board on this. I mean, how did this happen? How did a big name like Ellen Ross suddenly wake up one day and decide she wanted to play the part of Zelda Fitzgerald? She's never even mentioned the Fitzgerald project before. It's just the weirdest thing in the world. This wasn't going to be a major motion picture, you know. It was supposed to be more of an art-house thing, limited release in the theaters, a debut at Cannes or Sundance, and then maybe Netflix or Paramount + might buy the exclusive rights. Now, suddenly, it's a prestige picture that's being talked about like it's going to be Oscar bait."

Jackson was going to love the sound of that, Willow thought. Then again, if this movie was going to be some kind of A-list project, Jackson became that much more of a long shot to get the role of Scott. Willow wondered if Zelda would get involved and try to persuade the casting director to hire Jackson.

Willow would have to make sure Jackson didn't blow his audition because if he did, Zelda might not be so persuasive with the director. Willow didn't want to get Zelda involved, anyhow, because she hated the thought of taking away somebody's free will. Zelda already did that with Ellen - she took away Ellen's free will to choose her next project. Not technically, of course, because Ellen chose to become Zelda Fitzgerald in her next film. But she didn't *really* make that choice because Zelda was so persuasive that Ellen was making a decision without even realizing exactly why that decision was made.

That was a borderline case, Willow knew. But if Willow actually wanted to make a spell that would induce the director to hire Jackson, that would be crossing the line. So she wouldn't do that.

And if Zelda was going to do it, she didn't want to know. She certainly didn't want Jackson to know if that would be how he would get the part. It would make him feel like crap.

The only thing Willow felt comfortable doing was creating a confidence spell so Jackson didn't feel like a failure going into the audition. That would be the best way to help him get the part.

So, that evening, Willow gathered a purple candle and some Eucalyptus oil. She meditated, burned the candle and chanted the words that would give Jackson the confidence that he could get the part.

Chapter Eighteen

Willow

The next day, Willow went over to Jackson's house to help him with his audition. She knew her spell had worked when she looked into his eyes. His posture was straight, his eyes were dancing, and his smile was genuine.

Zelda and Clara were obviously there with Willow, although Willow warned them not to distract her while she was working with Jackson. She explained to them, again, that there was no way she could talk to them while she was in the same room as Jackson. They agreed to behave themselves.

However, Clara was reluctant to agree to that because she had a problem with boundaries. She always had boundary issues in life, and she obviously had the same issues in death. She still didn't understand why it wasn't appropriate for Willow to talk to her while other people were in the room.

"So people think you're screwy, so what?" Clara had asked.

Willow had rolled her eyes. "I know you don't understand, and, quite frankly, I really don't care if you understand or not. I only need you to know that if you talk to me, I won't answer you. I won't even look at you. Fair warning."

Clara had pouted, but she agreed not to talk to Willow while Willow was busy with Jackson. Zelda also agreed because Zelda did understand exactly why Willow couldn't talk to her when she was in the same room as Jackson. She didn't like it, either, because she absolutely hated to be ignored. That was her thing in life - she always wanted to be in the center of it all. But she understood, so she gave Willow her word that she wouldn't talk to her while she was in the room with Jackson.

"What if you guys start necking?" Clara had asked. "Can we watch?"

Willow got impatient at that moment. "Again, I'm not interested in him in that way."

"The bank's closed, then?" Clara had asked.

"What does that mean?" Willow had asked.

"It means you aren't interested in kissing him," Zelda had said.

"Yeah. The bank's closed," Willow had said.

Jackson gave her a big hug. "Willow, I can't tell you how excited I am you're going to help me with this audition. When I heard the news that Ellen Ross would be involved in this project, I got bummed. I just thought that now the movie would be a big deal, and obviously, the director was going to try to find a big name for the role of Scott. I didn't think the director would even look at a guy like me to star alongside the hottest actress in the world."

"But now you have a different attitude?" Willow asked him.

Jackson nodded his head. "It was so weird. Last night, at about 8 o'clock, I suddenly thought I'd get this part. It was like I got this burst of confidence, and I started to think I'd be a front-runner for the part. It was so strange. My brain was still telling me I was the longest of long shots. But my gut was telling me I was really going to impress the director, and he'd hire me."

That was all Willow needed to hear. Her spell had worked, and Jackson would go into the audition brimming with confidence. And he had a good chance of getting the part, as long as he had the attitude that the director would love him.

"Well, let's go through some lines."

So, for the rest of the day, Willow played Zelda to Jackson's Scott. Zelda herself was in the corner of the room, not saying anything, but she was making faces that were distracting to Willow.

Willow wanted to tell Zelda to quit making those faces. Of course, Willow wasn't doing the Zelda part justice. Willow wasn't an actress, after all. She was an alternative healer. Somehow, Zelda wanted her to be all these things she wasn't - a screenwriter, an actress, a woman in love with Jackson.

It was getting extremely annoying.

At some point, Jackson left the apartment because he was going to get some food and bring it back. "I'm gonna pick up some stuff at the organic restaurant down the street," Jackson told Willow. "What would you like?"

"Anything. I'm really not picky, and I like to be surprised. So just pick up anything, and I'll eat it and probably like it."

Willow actually preferred it when people picked out food for her occasionally. It got her out of her box, and it got her to try different food. She discovered some of her favorite dishes that way.

While Jackson was gone, Willow looked over at Clara and Zelda. "I know, I know, I suck. You don't have to say it, Zelda. I know you're thinking that."

Clara started to laugh. "Suck? I didn't notice you doing that to that boy."

Oh, that's right. When Clara and Zelda were kicking around, the word "suck" meant to give fellatio. "No, in this case, suck means bad. As in, I'm a terrible actress."

Zelda just shook her head. "I wasn't thinking that. I mean, you're right, you're not very good. I know you'll be a better writer than an actress, however. But I thought Jackson was extremely good. I was watching him, and it was almost like I was watching my Scott coming back to life."

The scene that Willow and Jackson were working on was a scene of Zelda and Scott early in their marriage. When they were young and just married, they were the toast of New York. Scott was a celebrity, and Zelda was, too, by extension. They were the golden couple that everybody wanted to be around.

It was said that Scott was the first writer to really capture New York during that golden period when the Jazz Age was just beginning, the building boom was happening, and the character of the city was changing from the aristo-cratic city of Edith Wharton novels to the booming metropolis it was becoming. Scott captured lightning in a bottle, making him the most celebrated writer of his day.

Scott was the one who chronicled the way young people were changing at that time. The world was transitioning from the Victorian Age to the Jazz Age, and Scott was the one who introduced the rest of the country to this change through his short stories and his novels. Because Scott, in a way, embodied the city in the early 1920s, the influence he had on New York City was outsized. Zelda was along for the ride, although she tried her best to stake her claim in New York society.

The scene Jackson was working on took place during this heady time - before the cheating, before the alcoholism, before the nervous breakdown, before Scott's depression and overwhelming fear of failure. Before Scott's health issues and Zelda's tragic death in a sanitarium.

Zelda nodded her head. "When I watched Jackson, I was taken back to those days. Those heady days, full of promise and color, when all our tomorrows were in front of us. Those early days when I thought we could never go wrong." Zelda started to cry. "I'm sorry. I didn't think it would be so profound and emotional to see the two of you acting out our early days. I haven't really thought about those days so much. It's really difficult to see it acted out in this way."

Willow was worried about Zelda's reaction to watching her act with Jackson. Zelda was obviously getting extremely nostalgic and emotional. Willow wondered if Zelda was going to be able to be a good screen-writing partner after all. It was going to be a bit of a problem because Zelda obviously had a perspective that might be different than the actual truth. Not just because Zelda ended up delusional and not in touch with reality, but also because Zelda saw her life with Scott with a biased eye.

No matter. Willow had already committed herself to writing this screenplay, and she'd already told Zelda she would tell her story the way Zelda wanted it told. She was going to see it through, no matter what.

Clara decided to give her two cents on the matter. "Willow, I don't think you were so bad. You're a little stiff, that's true, but you can work that out."

"Thanks, Clara, but I really don't care if I'm stiff or not. This isn't my career, and it never will be."

Just then, Jackson came back. "Here. I got you a burger made of tempeh."

Willow smiled. She actually loved tempeh burgers. Jackson did well in choosing the meal that would make Willow happy.

She took the burger from Jackson and bit into it. It was made with vegan mayonnaise, lettuce, tomato, and red onions. Jackson also got some French fries, and Willow was also happy with them. In Willow's book, there was no such thing as a bad French fry, nor such thing as too much garlic, nor such thing as bad pizza. Because even bad French fries and bad pizza were good in Willow's book.

Jackson sat down next to Willow. "I'm really glad you came to help me out. I don't know. There's something about you that makes me feel extremely calm. I feel like I can really make a go of this silly Hollywood game with you by my side. I know that sounds ridiculous because we don't know each other too well."

Willow took a fry, dragged it through some ketchup, and took a bite out of her tempeh burger. She wasn't going to address Jackson's obvious ardor for her. "You'll get the part, dude. And you're gonna knock it out of the park. When you're done with this movie, critics will say that Emma Ross was supposed to be the film's star, but you ran away with it. And you're going to be on your way from there."

Jackson was just staring at her. "You know what, I actually believe you. That's so weird. Before you came to town, I was really feeling like a failure. I thought I'd become a full-time Uber driver before everything was said and done. But, for the first time in a long time, I believe my big break is around the corner. And I think my big break just might be this movie."

"I think it will be," Willow said. "Now, after dinner, do you want to go through some more lines?"

"Not really. I think we've done enough. I thought it might be fun to go to the Santa Monica pier. It's not something I do all the time, but I always enjoy myself when I go there."

"Okay, sounds good."

So, they finished their burgers and then got in Jackson's car, a new BMW convertible in candy apple red, and headed down to the Santa Monica pier.

"Dude," Willow said when she got a look at his car. "If this is the car you drive, why the hell are you worried about becoming an Uber driver for your life?"

Jackson smiled as he drove along. "I told you, I've made a good name for myself in modeling. I get quite a few jobs. But modeling is a limited-time deal, and there are always younger and better-looking guys coming up. It's just a matter of time before my modeling agent stops finding work for me, and I'm just another piece of roadkill. And once that happens, if I don't have an acting career, it'll be a matter of time before I'm driving people around for a living. Not that there's anything wrong with that, but it's not what I want for my life."

Willow could understand that.

They arrived at the Santa Monica pier and, miraculously, found a parking spot on the street.

The Santa Monica pier had a distinct carnival

atmosphere about it. The famous Ferris wheel and roller coaster were on the pier, along with various shops, restaurants, and bars. There was also a massive aquarium and arcades. It was almost like a tiny Coney Island.

Willow had been to the Santa Monica pier before and always enjoyed herself when she went. The place reminded her of other places she had visited that had the same colorful carnival vibe, such as Myrtle Beach, South Carolina and Niagara Falls.

Jackson and Willow rode the roller coaster and the Ferris wheel. While they were on the Ferris wheel, the sun was setting on the water - a brilliant red and purple that blanketed the sky. Zelda and Clara were along for the ride, and Zelda especially got excited about the beauty of the sky. That was always her thing, sunsets. She liked to describe them in very poetic language. And there was something brilliant about this particular sunset, so Willow knew Zelda was really getting into this trip.

Willow heard Zelda sigh next to her. "Sometimes I get very sad when the evening falls like this with so much brilliant color. It makes me think about the early days with Scott and the sunsets we always enjoyed in New York. How different the sunsets were in New York from the ones in Alabama when I was growing up. New York, with all those enormous buildings, it was like the color had seeped into every crack in the sidewalk. But in Alabama, it was more like those trees were haunting us with their limbs in the dark. It was a completely different world, going from Alabama to New York. And I was such a different person in each of those places."

Zelda seemed like she wanted to tell Willow her story right there. But Willow didn't want to hear her story right at that moment. Willow wanted to concentrate on Jackson, who was next to her on the Ferris wheel and staring at her the entire time.

After a moment, however, Willow started to feel extremely uncomfortable. She felt the pull of being next to her soulmate, and she wanted to avoid that. So, after a few moments of looking into Jackson's gray-blue eyes, she looked away and out at the surf below.

"Look at those crazy people swimming in that cold water without a wetsuit," Willow said, pointing down to the few swimmers in the water. The late-April night air was cool, probably only around 60°, and Willow imagined the water was even colder. Willow shivered just thinking about being in the water below.

Jackson didn't say anything but just nodded his head. "Willow, I can't help this. I feel so connected to you. I don't even know what it is, but I feel like I'm coming home when I'm next to you. I sound like such a dope, talking like this."

"Well, dude, if you feel like a dope talking to me like that, then you're going to nail the part of Scott Fitzgerald tomorrow. Because that's exactly what he was, a lovestruck puppy who he felt he'd met his soulmate when he met Zelda. So just take that feeling you have sitting next to me and permeate your artistic vision of Scott with that emotion."

"I will," Jackson said, his face getting closer and closer to Willow's. "God, I have this overwhelming desire to kiss you."

Willow closed her eyes, and Jackson's lips met hers. The second their lips met, Willow felt the spark of electricity coursing through her body. She felt like every cell was being lit up inside her. And she knew from Jackson's reaction that he was feeling the same way.

Willow lost her breath. No. This was so wrong. This wasn't what was supposed to happen when she came out here.

But, then again, how could things have gone any other way?

Ever the romantic, Clara Bow watched the two of them with her big brown eyes dancing and an enormous smile on her bow-shaped lips. "I knew you'd fall in love with that fella," she said with a sigh. "He's dreamy. And I think he's in love with you. God, I wish I had a boy in love with me like that. Truth is, I fell in love with a new fella every week, sometimes two or three at the same time. But Zelda knew love like yours."

Willow tried to block out the sound of Clara's voice as she sat there on the Ferris wheel with Jackson. It was very difficult, however, because Clara was, once again, determined that Willow would acknowledge her. Willow was just as determined not to.

Jackson kissed her again, and Willow, once again, felt she was underwater and couldn't breathe. She never had felt so alive in her entire life. All she wanted was to stop time so that she and Jackson could stay on the Ferris wheel forever. The night air was crisp and cool, and the lights of the Santa Monica pier were dazzling and bright.

Willow finally cocked her head. "Tomorrow, I predict your life is going to change. By the end of the week, you'll get a call from the director, and you'll get that part. And, all at once, everybody's going to know your name."

That was like Scott Fitzgerald, too. Like Jackson, Scott had struggled for a long time with self-doubt and fear of failure. Before his first novel was published, he was convinced he would never make anything of himself. Then his novel was published, and, just like that, he was a celebrity. He was suddenly designated as the voice of a generation.

Jackson wasn't going to quite have that level of success with this part. His playing the part of Scott Fitzgerald wouldn't change the world like Scott's novels and short stories did. Yet, Willow knew that he would become famous after he got this part. He would come out of nowhere, so everybody would assume he was an overnight sensation. Of course, considering he'd been in Hollywood for six years, not really getting any traction, he wouldn't be an overnight sensation. But it was going to seem like he was because this was going to be his first real role, and it was going to be opposite the hottest actress in the world. So Jackson was on his way to becoming a phenom, and he would do it in his very first major role.

The Ferris wheel finally stopped, Willow and Jackson got off, and Jackson smiled as he went over to a game. It was one of those games where you had to put a ring on a bottle, and Jackson was, of course, very good. He won a large stuffed animal, a dog with an enormous hat. Willow was hoping he wouldn't win anything for her, as she didn't have a place in her house where a giant stuffed animal would look good. But she was happy to take the prize, anyhow.

The two walked along the boardwalk, Willow with her stuffed animal under her arm, Jackson holding her hand. It occurred to her that their time together just being like this, anonymous, with nobody recognizing Jackson, was going to soon come to an end. Once this movie came out and Jackson became a smash, the anonymity would be gone.

In fact, Willow had a good idea that just getting the part would take away Jackson's anonymity. The trade papers would run stories about him and show his picture because he would be this unknown getting this major role. He would have to get a publicist, who would ensure he was seen at the right places at the right time, so everybody would know about him before the movie came out.

Willow looked at Jackson and was tempted to tell him that he needed to savor this moment because his life was about to change. But she knew that he probably wouldn't understand. He wouldn't know what she was talking about, because, unlike her, he wasn't sensitive to changes in the universe. He wasn't aware of the moments when the universe decides to work on your behalf instead of always working against you. Thus far, Jackson had only experienced the feeling that everything was working against him. That was because, before, for whatever reason, Jackson wasn't ready for this moment.

But now he was. Willow could see this clearly now. The veil around Jackson, which had caused Willow to not be able to read him or the events around him, was coming down because Willow had finally realized she was fighting a losing battle. There was no reason to deny what was obvious to both of them – they were meant to be together. And once Willow decided to stop fighting that, she could see clearly just how things were changing for Jackson.

Jackson was looking at her with a smile on his face. "What are you thinking about?" he asked her.

Willow didn't tell him the truth. He wouldn't have understood, anyhow. Willow could tell him all day long exactly how his life would be once he got that part, but he wasn't going to understand it, so Willow didn't even try.

"Nothing, really. I was just kind of thinking it's been such a great day. That's all. I really like coming to places like the Santa Monica pier. It's like when I used to go to carnivals when I was a kid."

She wanted to tell him that she was still thinking about his kiss and how much she felt like she was on fire when he kissed her. But there was no way Willow would show her cards like that. She wasn't going to admit to Jackson, or anybody, for that matter, how she felt about him.

Jackson took a deep breath as they walked along the boardwalk. By now, it was nighttime, and the whole boardwalk was lit up in neon. Willow had been living on Nantucket for the better part of the past 10 years, and she hadn't really left the island very much during that time. Nantucket was a place where there was no neon. There was no modern architecture. There certainly wasn't a place where Willow could indulge her childlike fascination with carnival rides.

Now, Willow was out in California and wondered why she was so afraid to come out here. And Willow finally had to admit that she didn't want to come out here in the first place because of fear. That was why she initially told Zelda and Clara she wasn't going to come out to Los Angeles with them – she was afraid. She was afraid of her feelings for Jackson and that leaving the cocoon she was living in on Nantucket would make her feel vulnerable.

Willow never wanted to admit to herself she had a weakness. She always liked to tell herself that she was a badass who wasn't afraid of anything. Of course, that wasn't true. Willow knew that most people felt the same way she did. Most people who came off as badasses in their life were just as insecure and fearful of the world as people who seemed to be meek and mild. They just had a better way of covering up their apprehensions.

Willow thought about the story of Scott and Zelda. They were such a different couple - different from one another, that is. At least on the surface. Zelda was a girl who, growing up in Alabama, was considered the most popular girl in town. She had boys literally lined up for her at every dance. She had airmen who were stationed nearby do aerial maneuvers just to impress her. One guy who did this ended up badly injured in a crash. Zelda was bewitching all kinds of popular boys, from fraternity boys to captains of football teams. She just had everybody in that town eating out of her hands.

On the other hand, Scott was the kind of pitiful boy who invited a bunch of kids to his sixth birthday party, none of whom showed up. He ended up eating the big birthday cake his mother had made for him completely alone. That actually was one of the saddest stories Willow had ever read. Scott was so insecure that he wrote once that when he liked a guy, he wanted to become him - he literally wanted to shed his own skin to become the guy he admired. He definitely wasn't popular like Zelda. Even when he became the most celebrated writer in the world with the publication of his very first book, his insecurities never left him.

But were Zelda and Scott really all that different from one another in the end? In her life in Alabama, Zelda came off as the devil-may-care badass that covered up the fact that her family was dealing with a lot of mental illness - her older sister, Marjorie, ended up in a sanitarium. Her brother Tony killed himself because he had recurring dreams of killing his mother. Her mother was a free-spirited woman who had that free spirit quenched by the realities of bringing up a large family while being married to an oppressive man. Zelda pretended to shake all of that off, as her early life was marked by her own free-spirited attitude – she loved to roller-skate, climb trees, dive into lakes, play with the boys, and flirt with everybody in town. But she ended up in a sanitarium herself. She obviously had an outer shell that covered up her own insecurities.

Scott was different from Zelda in that he wore his insecurities on his sleeve. But really, the attraction between them wasn't just intellectual, but it was also the meeting of two wounded souls. Zelda just pretended to the world her soul wasn't wounded when it so obviously was. Scott never pretended his soul wasn't wounded. That wound made him a great writer but a lousy person who had no qualms in plagiarizing his wife and drank away his days of failure.

Willow, in a way, had something in common with Zelda. Like Zelda, she came off to the rest of the world like a free-spirited badass who couldn't care less about what other people thought of her. Anybody who knew Willow thought she was a woman who had the world at her feet. But she knew the truth, and it was staring at her in the face in the form of Jackson. The truth was, she was incomplete without him. But just thinking those words in her head made her want to vomit. God, she didn't want to give up her independence. She cherished that more than anything in the world.

But she also knew Jackson wouldn't demand her to relinquish her independence. He wasn't going to control her, tell her what to do, keep her in a box and try to quench her spirit the way Scott did to Zelda. She knew he wouldn't take away her essence because he never did that to her in all their other lives together. It just wasn't in him.

"Willow," Jackson said to her. "Why am I feeling you're going to play a big part in this movie I'm hopefully going for?" He shook his head as if he was getting some kind of a vision or something, but he wasn't sure what it was and wasn't sure if he could trust it.

Willow wasn't ready to tell him the truth about her working on the screenplay for Nancy. She suddenly felt the pull to stay in Los Angeles because she wanted to stay close to him. But she certainly wasn't going to tell him that either. Willow thought if she told Jackson the truth that she was getting involved in writing screenplays, even at a ghost-writing level, he would suddenly get the idea that she was meant to be out in Los Angeles with him. And she wasn't quite willing to go there just yet.

"Not sure why you're thinking I'm going to be involved with your project. Maybe because I was your scene partner today, you think I want to be a part of the movie. But, trust me, I don't. My life is across the country on a tiny little island where nothing much happens."

Jackson just shook his head. "Huh. Okay, if you say so. Anyhow, what do you want to do next?"

Willow knew what she wanted to do. She wanted to be with him that night, feel close to him, and have him make love to her. She knew he wanted the same thing. She could tell it in his eyes and feel it in his touch.

She closed her eyes, trying to will away the feelings washing over her like the ocean waves raging below the pier. She wasn't going to give in to her lust for this man. And she certainly wasn't going to give in to her love for the man. She knew she would never want to leave the city if she did. And where would that leave her? It would leave her without the business she'd worked hard to build over the years. It would leave her in a strange city known for swallowing people whole and spitting them out. Los Angeles was the city where so many dreams came to die. Willow didn't want to be counted as one of its casualties.

"Actually, I'm getting a little bit tired."

Clara, who up until this moment was uncharacteristically quiet, suddenly wasn't so quiet. "What are you doing?

That fella's in love with you, and you're trying to tell him the bank is closed. You open that bank, or you'll be sorry."

Willow shot a look at Clara, and Jackson noticed it.

"Willow, are you okay? I didn't want to say anything earlier, but I swear to God you're always looking at something that isn't there. And just now, you gave the biggest stink eye to that lamppost." Then he smiled. "I have no idea what that lamppost did to piss you off, but after seeing how you looked at it, I'm never going to piss you off, that's for sure."

Great. Willow really thought Jackson wasn't noticing all the looks she was giving to both Clara and Zelda during her day there with Jackson, but he was much more perceptive than she gave him credit for. He wasn't thick as a bowling ball, as Clara would say.

Willow just shrugged her shoulders. "I don't know what you're talking about."

She closed her eyes as Clara was, once again, babbling in her ear. "He wants you to neck with him. He wants you to make whoopee with him. He's goofy over ya, and you're giving him the bum's rush."

Zelda, thankfully, intervened. "Clara, you need to stop bothering Willow about this. She shouldn't be forced into doing something she doesn't want to do just because you want her to."

Willow was grateful that Zelda was putting Clara in her place, but, damn, it was hard to concentrate on Jackson with those two bickering ghosts so close to her ear. A part of her wanted to admit to Jackson what she was going through at that moment. She knew he'd understand if she told him the truth. But there was still something holding her back.

There was still a lingering fear that he'd think she was

nuts if she admitted to him that she was being followed by the spirits of two notable women of the 1920s.

Willow just finally put her foot down. "Jackson, your audition is tomorrow. I think you need to go home and try to get some sleep. But I want you to call me as soon as your audition is over because I want to know how it goes. Okay?"

Jackson looked very disappointed, but he nodded his head and squeezed her hand. "You're right. I need my sleep this night, of all nights. I can't go into the audition dragging ass."

Willow knew what he was thinking. The more she realized she wanted to be with him, the more she was able to get on his wavelength. And he thought that if she were there tonight, he would be calmed down. He would actually sleep better if she were there. Even if she was sleeping on his couch, he would definitely get a better night's sleep if she were around.

But would they be able to just stay the night in the same apartment without climbing into bed together? Willow doubted it.

Although it was against her better judgment, she made the offer she knew he was looking for. "Okay. I'll come and stay with you tonight. But I want to make one thing perfectly clear. I'm going to spend the night on your couch. I don't want you to be chivalrous and insist I sleep on the bed while you sleep on the couch. I don't want to spend the night with you in the same bed. I want to be there in the apartment for you because I think you need me to be."

His face brightened up when she said that. "I'd love for you to come over and spend the night, even if you just spend the night on the couch. I really want you near, because tomorrow is the biggest day of my entire life. And there's just something about you that calms me down. But I want to do what you just asked me not to and sleep on the couch while you get the bed."

Willow shook her head vigorously. "I'm telling you, Jackson, if that's what you're going to do, bug me to take your bed, the deal's off. You need to sleep in your bed tonight. You're the one who has a big audition tomorrow. I don't have anything going on tomorrow, so I'm not the one who needs to get a good night of restorative sleep."

Jackson nodded, but Willow knew he didn't like her terms. He was naturally a very chivalrous and polite guy who would literally give his shirt off his back to somebody who needed it and who would ordinarily give up his bed and be uncomfortable on the couch in such a situation they were about to be in. But Willow wasn't going to have it, and he knew it.

"It won't be too bad. My couch is pretty comfortable."

Willow smiled, and he put his arm around her as they walked along. His touch felt safe, comforting.

The two of them got to his apartment, and he gave her a big T-shirt to sleep in. It was late, almost midnight, and his audition was at 9 o'clock in the morning. Willow insisted that he get right to bed, and he did, with reluctance.

After he went to the bedroom, Clara started talking to Willow. "Aw, I wish you would join that fella, but I know why you don't. You want to make sure he gets that part. I think you're goofy over him, just like he's goofy over you."

Willow knew that the word "goofy," as Clara used it, meant Willow was in love with him, and he was in love with her.

"Yes," Willow admitted to Clara. "I'm definitely goofy. And he is too."

Clara smiled big. "I knew it."

"Yes, you're right. Now please, go and find some all-night nightclub where you can go crazy, dance, and do whatever you want. And take Zelda with you. I really need to get some sleep myself."

"We're going, we're going," Clara said. "You're giving us the bum's rush, but that's okay."

They disappeared, and Willow looked at the ceiling.

She really was goofy. And so was Jackson.

And that scared the hell out of her.

Chapter Nineteen

Sarah

The next day, after the dinner where Julia and Sarah agreed they would move out to Los Angeles together, they went down to the beach with Mary. Max was very tired, so he was taking a nap while the two ladies and Julia went down to the beach together. Sarah called Ava to join them, and Ava would soon be there as well.

It was a beautiful day. Late April was typically a sunny day in California. "May Grey" and "June Gloom," which referred to the relentlessly overcast days that marked most of May and June in Southern California, were not quite upon them. Also typical of Southern California during the summer months was zero rainfall. But April, and early spring, were months where there might be a rain storm or two, which were most welcome in a state that had been in a perpetual drought for many years.

The beach below Mary's home, which was at the bottom of a large cliff, was private. It could only be accessed by people who lived in the adjoining neighborhood, so it wasn't as crowded as many other beaches would be at that time.

Mary had a couple of extra surfboards and a surfboard for herself. Julia smiled because she'd told Sarah that she loved to surf. Sarah, herself, also loved to surf. Fortunately, Mary also had several wetsuits hanging up in her closet, two of which fit Sarah and Julia perfectly.

Sarah got to a spot on the beach where they could stake their claim. She planted an umbrella in the sand, set some beach chairs up underneath the umbrella, and called Ava to tell her where they would be. And then, Julia, Mary, and Sarah all took their surfboards out to the middle of the ocean and waited for some waves to ride.

Sarah loved being on the water. It was where she felt the most free. Studies had been done about the effect of a body of water on people's psyches. These studies found that being around a body of water, such as an ocean or a lake, had a very calming effect on people. Water tended to slow down people's heart rates and reduce stress hormones.

Sarah knew these studies were correct. She knew it in her bones. It was why it was so desirable to live on the coast. It was why beach houses cost so much money -they were desirable because people were just attracted to living by the water.

It was why she loved living in Monterey. Her house there was right on a beach. So, even though she was in a toxic relationship with a controlling man, she could escape her situation by going down to the beach, inhaling the air, and listening to the waves.

She wanted to find a beach house there in California. She hoped she could afford one. The house she just bought on Nantucket was valued at just under $2 million. If she sold it, she might be able to afford a small bungalow on one of the Los Angeles beaches. The beach communities in California tended to be populated by surfers and stoners who were renting homes. Sarah wasn't thrilled about the prospect of raising Julia in such an environment, so she would have to be careful about what neighborhood she would settle in.

Sarah, Mary, and Julia lay on the surfboards, waiting for the waves. Sarah looked over at Julia, who looked so cute in her hot pink and black shorty wetsuit. Julia looked over at Sarah and smiled. "Waves aren't great right now," she shouted at Sarah.

"I know, just be patient," Sarah shouted back.

Finally, a large wave was forming behind them, and Sarah paddled furiously as the wave swept her along. She stood up on the board, feeling like she was flying through the air, her arms straight out, her strong legs firmly planted. This was a great wave because it took Sarah all the way to the shore. She wished she could feel that way always - like she was weightless. Like she could be airborne.

Like Sarah, Mary and Julia also seemed to be expert surfers. They rode several waves all the way to the shore, both staying upright and not wiping out.

Sarah wasn't born close to an ocean. She wasn't raised by one, either. In fact, for the first 22 years of her life, she lived in the Midwest. She was raised in Kansas City and attended undergraduate school at the University of Kansas in Lawrence. However, when she was very young, she usually visited beaches in South Carolina, such as Folly Beach, the closest beach to Charleston, and Myrtle Beach, the famous beach with the same kind of carnival atmosphere she experienced on the Santa Monica pier.

On the way from Charleston to Myrtle Beach, which

was about a 2-hour drive, Sarah, Ava, and their uncle Nick, the uncle who usually took them out to the coast, stopped by Murrell's Inlet, where they got the freshest seafood Sarah had ever tasted. Unfortunately, Sarah found the seafood she got there in California didn't compare to the seafood she got in South Carolina.

During her trips out to South Carolina, Sarah learned to surf. When she was very young, she was always terrified of it, but her uncle Nick encouraged her to try. She became a part of the small group of girls who stood around in a circle, listening to some older surfers explain how to paddle the surfboard and balance on it. She was only seven years old the first time she caught a wave and rode it in, and she was hooked. She, Ava, and Nick returned to South Carolina time and again over the next 10 years. Every time she returned to South Carolina, she got better and better on the board.

She knew she wanted to live in California after graduating from her undergraduate school in Kansas. She was thrilled to have been accepted at Berkeley, which was only about 1/2 an hour away from several beaches. She studied hard and did extremely well at Berkeley, but she and a group of her friends always went to the beaches on the weekends. They also went to wineries on the weekends, including several in Berkeley, along with taking day trips to Napa Valley and Sonoma, which were about an hour away from Berkeley.

Sarah loved living in Berkeley when she was going to school there. It was a heady time of freedom, surfing, wineries, and looking forward to a bright future. Of course, her future didn't turn out so bright for her, as she made the mistake of quitting her architectural job to follow a controlling and volatile man around the world.

Now, she seemed to be given a second chance to make things right. She had the chance over 20 years ago to live her dream of living in California. She worked at a large architectural firm in Los Angeles, and the world was her oyster. Her Los Angeles life back then was cut short by her own mistakes. She wouldn't make the same mistake. She wouldn't ever give her life completely over to a man again.

She was going to concentrate on Julia, maybe try to find a job at a winery or a resort. The world was again going to be her oyster, and she would take full advantage of it.

Julia, Mary, and Sarah surfed for several hours. When they came in to sit under the umbrella, Ava was there. Sarah sat next to her, taking off her wetsuit, under which was a bikini, and put some more sunscreen on her body and face.

The three of them sat by the beach for the rest of the day, although Sarah went to check on Max several times. He slept most of the day, which Sarah knew was a bad sign. Cancer tended to take up a lot of energy, and as it advanced, it sapped out the lifeblood. When a cancer patient spent most of his or her time sleeping, it was a good indication the end was near.

Not that Max didn't have a chance to have another good day. There was always a chance he could rally. In fact, shortly before death, terminal patients often experience a burst of energy. They suddenly begin to talk a lot more, participate in activities they hadn't been able to before, and even recover their appetite. Sarah had a friend, Mia, who was in the last stages of pancreatic cancer. Her family was thrilled that she was hungry for sushi one day, and she seemed to be back to normal. Her husband was so thrilled about this that he posted her progress on Facebook, along with a picture of her sitting up in bed, a smile on her face and a plate of sushi on her tray. That posting got hundreds of likes and comments, as the people who loved Mia were excited she was getting better.

A day later, she went to sleep and never woke up. And that was what it was like for cancer patients. It wasn't like they would just be there one moment, awake and aware and dead the next. No, it was more a process of watching their loved one slip away during a period of days, as they would sleep without waking up, and, at some point, their breaths would become more and more shallow. There would be more and more time in between each breath.

And then, just like that, their breaths would be no more.

By the time the trio got in from the beach, it was around 6 o'clock, and the sun was still out. Max was in the kitchen, making dinner for everybody. Sarah was happy to see him up and about, but she worried. Was this the burst of energy before the rapid decline? Or was this just Max rallying a bit after getting some rest, which he clearly needed? Sarah hoped and prayed for the latter but was terrified it was the former.

"Hello, lovely," Max said to Sarah. He kissed her on the cheek. "I made some ginger Ono fish, with a baked potato and a green salad. I hope all of you ladies are hungry."

They were. They all sat down around the table on the back patio and enjoyed their meal with a bottle of wine.

Sarah loved sitting on the back patio. She loved smelling the flowers - the jasmine, the roses, the hibiscus that grew in a huge bush close to the patio. She was amused by the tiny lizards running wild throughout Southern California patios and backyards. And, in fact, if it weren't for the fact that Max was clearly not doing so well, Sarah would've really enjoyed herself during that dinner. The conversations were lively, the jokes were flying, and Julia was coming out of her shell. Ever since she informed Sarah that she wanted to stay there in California, and Sarah agreed, it seemed that something had lightened in Julia's demeanor, and she was much friendlier.

"I talked to Emerson today," Julia was saying excitedly. "She's so all about my coming out to Los Angeles to live. She was worried she wouldn't know anybody out here, so when I told her I'd be living out here, she was so here for it."

Max had a rueful smile on his face. It was clear he had mixed emotions about all of this. On the one hand, he was happy to see his daughter looking more joyful and energetic than she had in a while. The day at the beach and surfing had done Julia a world of good. Apparently, her conversation with her good friend Emerson also buoyed her spirits.

On the other hand, he wouldn't be able to see Julia become a woman. He wouldn't be able to experience her joy at living on the West Coast on a beach. And that loss showed on his face.

That evening, Max and Sarah did the dishes, while Ava, Julia, and Mary played a board game and chatted around the patio table. Max wanted to talk to Sarah alone, which was why they were doing the dishes, just the two of them.

"I'm going to see a doctor tomorrow," he said. "I fully expect the doctor will give me what I need, which is a diagnosis of terminal cancer with less than six months to live."

Sarah slowly ran her sponge around the plate and put it into the dishwasher. "Okay," she said. "I'll come with you, of course."

He nodded his head. "The thing is, the doctor I'm seeing at UCLA is a renowned specialist in treating melanoma. He's a doctor who has been known to take hopeless patients and treat them to where they go into remission."

Sarah looked at Max. She felt a little flutter of hope for the first time since she found out about his terminal diagnosis. What was he trying to say to her? He'd told her that several of his doctors had given him very little time.

"I don't understand," Sarah said. "Are you saying there might be a chance after all?"

Max nodded his head. "I didn't want to say anything to anybody. I don't want to get anybody's hopes up. But a lot of the times when I've been in the room alone, I sleep a lot, but when I'm awake, I get on the computer and do a ton of research on my illness. I know I've said I'm ready to give up, but I'm not."

Sarah's ears perked up. She didn't want to get her hopes up, that was for sure. But maybe there was a chance?

"There's a certain treatment a doctor out in UCLA has been pioneering," Max said. "He is the best in the world at using immunotherapy and targeted therapy for advanced melanoma patients. I was so lucky to actually get an appointment with him."

Sarah was actually quite well-versed in immunotherapy. When Nolan was sick, Sarah spent her time looking at studies about treating the disease. Many of the studies she read dealt with the topic of immunotherapy, which was simply using the body's natural immunity system as part of a treatment protocol. It was very effective in slowing down the progression of ALS in some cases. Unfortunately for Nolan, it didn't work for him.

"You know, about 6% of hospice patients actually get better and get out of hospice," Sarah said. That was significant because, to qualify for hospice, you must have a terminal diagnosis and be given less than six months to live. The fact that 6% of people are given a terminal diagnosis and enter hospice care but get well enough to come out of hospice meant that there were people who were given terminal diagnoses but got better.

Max nodded his head. "Don't say anything to anybody. I'm only telling you because I really need to talk to somebody. And you told me how much you did research for your ex-boyfriend's disease. If you want to, I'd like you to do the same thing for me if the doctor tells me there might be a chance I could beat this thing."

Sarah nodded her head. "Yes. I'd actually like to be part of your team if there is any chance at all that you could maybe be cured."

Max laughed. "I thought about talking to Mary about this, but she's a hippie-dippy artist who knows absolutely nothing about medicine or science. As much as I love her, I don't know if I can rely on her as my research buddy. I think I can ask you to do that, and you'll do well with that role."

"I will." Sarah took a deep breath. She didn't want to think there was a possibility that Max might get better. She didn't want to get her hopes up and be disappointed. She wanted to talk to Max's new doctor, ask some questions, and get a better idea about Max's chances before she started thinking that he might end up being the man she spent her life with.

And, as much as Sarah didn't want to admit it, there was also a sense of fear about the prospect that Max might get better. She'd be thrilled if there was a miracle and Max could beat this thing. At the same time, she was married to him and still didn't really know him. She assumed when she married him on a whim in Vegas, and he told her he didn't have much time left, things were going to go on a trajectory where he was going to pass in a matter of months, and

Sarah was going to take care of his daughter Julia after his passing.

But if things took a turn, suddenly, everything would look different for Sarah. She would have to overcome her fear of giving up her freedom. She feared being in a relationship with a man meant she would be controlled and subsumed again. She was going to be part of a family unit, and she wasn't sure how she felt about that.

Then, she immediately felt guilty for even thinking along those lines. She needed to be nothing but happy if Max was able to somehow get a treatment that would cure him. She needed to put aside any kind of misgivings about the possibility that Max would be in her life for much longer than she had anticipated.

Max seemed to read her mind. "Sarah," he said, "there's not much of a chance I can beat this thing. My cancer is pretty well advanced. But if I do recover, I guess you and I will have to reassess our relationship. I know we married on a whim, and it was my idea to do it. I want you to know you're not stuck in this relationship if things improve for me."

Sarah was impressed that he could read her mind, but, at the same time, she wondered if he was trying to back out of their relationship. Perhaps *he* didn't really want to be married to *her.* Or maybe, like herself, he was apprehensive because he didn't know her well enough to know if he wanted to be married to her. Maybe he was just hedging his bets.

"We'll cross that bridge when we come to it," Sarah said. "In the meantime, I'll go to your doctor's appointment with you tomorrow and see what they say. I'm assuming they have all the medical records from your Boston doctors?" Max had been treated in Boston for his illness because Nantucket didn't have any kind of advanced medical center on the island, let alone the kind of specialists that would be needed to effectively treat his kind of advanced cancer.

"Of course. This new doctor has all my medical records, so he can give me a good indication tomorrow if there's a chance for me."

Sarah finished up the dishes and then kissed Max on the cheek. Thus far, they hadn't made love even one time. This was partly because of his illness and partly because, ironically enough, they didn't know each other well enough to become intimate.

Sarah hadn't been with a man intimately since Nolan. She wondered if she would be able to make love with a man because she wondered if she could get over the memories of her toxic 20-plus-year relationship for long enough to want to make love to somebody. She was very attracted to Max, but Sarah had to have more than physical attraction before she was willing to make love to a man. She needed to be loved, thoroughly and totally, and for that to happen, she needed to feel that she was seen and that the man knew her inside and out.

Max and Sarah joined the others on the patio. They were laughing and joking, and Ava and Mary were becoming fast friends over their bottle of wine. They were playing a game of Monopoly, and Julia seemed to be winning, as she had several townhouses on some high-dollar properties like Park Place and Boardwalk. Mary, whose piece was the little dog, was in jail. It was Ava's turn on the board, and she landed on Park Place and had to pay Julia a lot of money. She just laughed and cheerfully dispensed the Monopoly money to young Julia.

"Hey," Ava said to Sarah and Max as they came out on

the back patio. "Julia here is a shark, I tell you," Ava said with a twinkle in her eye.

Max and Sarah watched the rest of the game, and everybody had a great night.

Sarah was going to have to talk to Ava about Max. Ava would be able to give her good advice, she knew. At least, Sarah would have to clue Ava in if Max got good news from his doctor tomorrow.

All of a sudden, things were looking different. On the one hand, if Max had hope, everything might get better for him and Julia.

On the other hand, if Max got better, Sarah would have to decide. Did she really want to be married to him?

That was a question she didn't think she would have to face. But, there it was. There was a slight possibility that she would have to face it.

She really didn't know what the answer was going to be.

Chapter Twenty

Willow

Jackson's audition was at 9 o'clock on Tuesday, and Zelda went with Jackson that day. "I want to be there because I'll be able to tell you how he did," Zelda explained. "I have high hopes because when he was running through his lines with you playing me, he was my Scott brought to life. I know he'll get the part if he can have that same spirit when he's in front of the casting director."

Clara, for her part, also wanted to go along on the audition. "I spent my best years in front of a camera, and I miss going to the movie studio. I really wanna see how things have changed since I was making movies."

So, the upshot was that Willow was alone in Jackson's apartment while Jackson was busy with his audition. It was the first time in a long time that Willow actually had time to think. It was the first time in a long time that she didn't have two bickering ghosts chattering away in her ear.

And, the weird thing was, she actually started to miss

those two crazy broads. She never thought she'd ever think that being by herself was a lonely endeavor. Before Clara and Zelda invaded her space, Willow was often alone. She didn't have a ton of close friends on the island. She liked Hallie a lot because Hallie was her business partner, and she was really cool. And, on occasion, she had dinner with Hallie's friends, Ava, Sarah, and Quinn. But, typically, she preferred solitude.

She was introverted. That was her basic nature. She socialized on occasion, but only when she was in the mood. But, most of the time, she preferred to use her spare time reading books, painting and sculpting, and sometimes binging on a Netflix or Hulu series that looked good to her.

In other words, she wasn't the kind of person who needed to have people around. She wasn't even the kind who *liked* to have people around. Yet, she found that when Clara and Zelda had left her, she'd gotten used to the constant chattering. She'd gotten used to Clara talking about her men, Zelda talking about her life with Scott, and the two of them bickering all the time.

Oh, boy, Willow thought. She wondered if she was now going to actually want the company of spirits around her. And then she wondered if Zelda and Clara were only the beginning. She imagined that Zelda would probably move on once the ghost told her story for the screenplay. She didn't necessarily think Zelda would move on to her final destination, although Willow knew that would be a possibility for Zelda. But Zelda also seemed to have the choice to stick around and influence the living, as she was doing with Willow.

Clara also had the same possibilities, although it was less clear exactly why Clara was sticking around. Maybe she wanted her story to be told. However, Willow thought that probably wasn't the case with Clara, as Clara didn't seem interested in forcing Willow to tell her story through a screenplay, a novel, or a biography. That was typical for Clara, Willow thought. In life, Clara seemed to just live from one day to the next. It wasn't like she even thought of her movies as a legacy for her - she thought of them as a fun way to make money. And when she was done with the movies, she was done. The fans still loved her and wanted her when she retired, but Clara had had enough, and that was that.

So, Willow wondered what would happen when the screenplay was finished, and Zelda no longer had a reason to hang around. When she moved on, would she take Clara with her? Or maybe Clara wanted to stay around there in Los Angeles, so she could be close to the movie industry. Willow didn't know the answer to that question, but she knew she was starting to like having them around.

Maybe Willow needed the company of others more than she thought. This entire scenario with Clara and Zelda made her realize she needed people.

She was also starting to realize, with Jackson, that maybe she needed love in her life as well.

At around 5 o'clock that day, Zelda returned to the hotel room with Clara. "I wanted to tell you how Jackson's audition went," Zelda said to Willow.

Truth be told, Willow was on pins and needles all day, wanting to get word on how Jackson did. She didn't want to admit how anxious she was that Jackson did well. She knew in her heart that he had knocked it out of the park. That was the message that the universe was sending to her. But she definitely wanted confirmation.

"Well, out with it," Willow said to Zelda.

Zelda seemed to sigh. "He made Scott come to life more than all the other actors auditioning. I watched all the auditions today, and Jackson was much better than any of them. I think your boyfriend is going to get the role."

"He's not my boyfriend," Willow said. "By the way, where's Clara?"

"Right here, toots," Clara said, making Willow jump. "Your fella, he was really the cat's pajamas today. I know he got the job. The casting director, he was really impressed. I bet Jackson gets the call from the casting director by the end of the week."

Jackson arrived back at the apartment about an hour after Clara and Zelda had arrived. It was the traffic in Los Angeles that delayed him so much. After all, Clara and Zelda were literally able to fly over from the audition. Being a mere mortal with a car in Los Angeles, Jackson wasn't so lucky.

He had in his arms a dozen roses and a bottle of champagne. He looked like he wanted to celebrate, but Willow knew he didn't know yet if he got the part.

"Things went really well today," Jackson said. "I auditioned with an actress you've probably never heard of. She was just a stand-in for the part of Zelda. But if I get a callback, I'll be auditioning with Ellen herself. They obviously want to know what kind of chemistry I'm going to have with her. But that's only if I get the callback."

He gave her the roses. "These are for you, for coming out here and keeping me company. Before you came, I was feeling very down. I felt like things just were never going to happen for me. I don't know. I haven't felt like that since you've been around. I went into that audition today thinking I could slay that dragon. And I think it's because of you."

Willow took the roses, which were in a crystal vase. "Thanks," she said to him. "Well, I've been hanging around here all day because I wanted to talk to you about your audition today. Now I found out, and I really gotta get going."

"Oh. I was hoping I could treat you to dinner. There's a great Chinese place just down the street. Nothing like greasy Chinese to top off a great day."

Willow felt like she was breaking down her walls with every moment she spent with Jackson. Not that that was something she wanted to do because it wasn't. She really wanted to get out of the apartment, leave Los Angeles and never return. What was so wrong with her life before? She was living life on her terms, not somebody else's, and she wasn't prepared to give that up.

Yet, she knew in her heart she would give all that up. She would give in to Jackson's pull, sooner or later. So she might as well just get it over with.

"Okay, let's go to your Chinese place," Willow said.

Chapter Twenty-One

Sarah

The next day, Sarah accompanied Max to his appointment with Dr. Quan. She'd spent the previous evening after she talked to Max doing research on Dr. Quan and his methods. It seemed he had a pretty good track record with patients who had advanced melanoma, even melanoma that had spread to the lungs and the brain, which was the case with Max.

Dr. Quan shook Max's hand, and smiled at Sarah and shook her hand as well. "It's very nice to meet both of you," he said. He was a very slight Asian man who apparently ran marathons, judging by the pictures in his office of him completing marathons with his arms raised triumphantly. "Now, Max, I've been extensively reviewing your medical history. I believe you are an excellent candidate for a clinical trial that will test some very powerful immunotherapy drugs that have shown much promise in cases like yours."

Dr. Quan then went on to describe the drugs that were

being used in the clinical trials. They were drugs that fell under the umbrella of monoclonal antibodies, which were created by cloning a unique white blood cell. Sarah knew something about this topic because monoclonal antibodies were one of the treatments Nolan received for his advanced ALS.

Sarah knew how to ask all the right questions. So, for the better part of the hour, Sarah asked Dr. Quan question after question about this clinical trial. She realized that this particular clinical trial was no guarantee whatsoever that Max would beat his cancer. Different people always react to different treatments in different ways. But Dr. Quan seemed to think that this particular clinical trial held the most promise for Max.

So, after the meeting with Dr. Quan, Max decided to go ahead and enroll in the clinical trial. He wanted to have the chance that he could actually be cured. Dr. Quan told him there was a chance he could be cured, outright cured, not just have his life prolonged. Max had confided to Sarah that he had no interest in a treatment that would extend his life by a matter of months or even years in exchange for not having any quality of life during these extra months or years. It just wasn't worth it to him. He said he considered such treatments to be prolonging death, not prolonging life.

But Dr. Quan was offering the chance for him to be cured. To have a long life free of cancer. To be able to walk Julia down the aisle when she got married, cheer for her when she graduated from college and high school, and meet any future grandchildren. Max didn't think any of that was possible, but Dr. Quan said it was. He cautioned them that it wasn't probable – Max still only had about a 20% chance of being cured of his cancer. But 20% was not nothing, which was what Max was looking at before he came to Los Angeles.

Max held Sarah's hand as they drove back to Mary's house. "I don't want to tell Mary and Julia about this, especially Julia. I just don't think she can take the emotional roller coaster."

"Well, Max, they're going to know. You're going to be receiving treatment that's going to make you very sick. I think you probably need to tell them the truth. Tell them there's a slight chance you'll be around. That you might live until a ripe old age. You're going to have to break the bad news to Julia that there's a possibility she'll have to find you a nursing home one day."

Max started to laugh. "I feel like we're getting ahead of ourselves. I've spent the last year and a half with this death sentence just hanging over my head like a Sword of Damocles. To tell you the truth, I don't know how to live another way. I guess I'm saying that I've been living like I was dying, like the song says, because that's what I thought was going to happen. I don't know how to live like I'm not dying."

Sarah put her hand on his shoulder. "I don't know what you mean when you tell me you've been living like you're dying. But if it means things like forgiving people who've wronged you, not sweating the small stuff, doing things on your bucket list, living every day like it's your last, and looking at the ocean and feeling incredibly small, then my advice to you is to keep doing that. Keep that same perspective on life even if you beat this thing. If you become cured, you can see this time as a gift. Your illness gave you the gift of a different perspective. All of us would love to have the perspective that all these things that seem so important to us really aren't."

Max smiled and squeezed her hand. "Thank you so much for everything you've done."

They arrived at Mary's home. Max was extremely fatigued, so he greeted Mary and Julia and then went to his bedroom for a nap. Sarah told Mary and Julia that she should probably get to her hotel room. Ava was hanging out at the hotel, and Sarah needed to talk to her. If anybody was going to be able to relate to her fears of her future and the guilt she felt for being afraid of what might happen to her life if Max miraculously became cured of his disease, it would be Ava.

Not only that, but Sarah wanted to escape the house. Something was foreboding about being there. Not that Mary didn't make Sarah feel welcome. On the contrary, Mary went out of her way to make Sarah feel very welcome. But there was just something about being in that house that Sarah needed to escape.

So, Sarah greeted Mary and then told her she would be at the hotel. "Give me a call if you want me to come over for dinner or a movie or whatever," Sarah said to Mary.

Mary nodded her head. "I will." She looked like she wanted to talk to Sarah some more, so Sarah stood there, waiting for Mary to address whatever was on her mind.

"How did the doctor's visit go?" Mary asked Sarah.

"It went fine," Sarah said. She didn't want to answer questions because Max told her to keep her mouth shut about the possibility that he had a chance to get better.

"Did the doctor give him what he needs to give to the death with dignity people?" Mary asked.

"Not exactly. I'm so sorry, but I can't talk about this."

Mary nodded her head. "I know. It's been very emotional for me, too. And for Julia."

Sarah didn't mean she couldn't talk about the doctor's

office because she was emotional. Rather, she couldn't talk about it because Max didn't want her to. But she let Mary believe that she didn't want to say anything because she was just too emotional about it all.

Sarah said goodbye to Mary. Julia was apparently at the beach, surfing with some friends.

And then Sarah returned to her hotel room so she could talk to Ava about all of her feelings.

Chapter Twenty-Two

Willow

Willow ended up spending the night with Jackson the night that he took her out for some Chinese food to celebrate his successful audition. And the two of them ended up kissing on the couch. Clara and Zelda, thankfully, were nowhere to be found when Willow and Jackson ended up making out like two teenagers.

Willow had no idea where the two ghosts went, but she was happy to have the night away from them. This was the first time since she had been out in Los Angeles that she could focus on Jackson without the running commentary and bickering of the two ghosts. She was going to make the most of the opportunity.

The next day, Willow found out what the deal was. Jackson already had a call back from the casting director. He was supposed to meet with the director and Emma Ross that following Friday - in two days' time.

" Wow," Jackson said when he got off the phone with

the casting director. "I didn't think I would get a call back this soon, and I didn't think my next audition was going to be so soon."

By then, Zelda and Clara were back in the apartment. And Zelda explained exactly why Jackson got a call back so soon. Zelda told Willow that she had visited the director, Hal Lombard, who was an A-List director, during the night. She told him Jackson was meant to play the part of Scott Fitzgerald. So, as with Emma Ross, Hal Lombard probably woke up thinking about the craziest dream he had about Zelda Fitzgerald herself talking up Jackson Flynn for the role of Scott Fitzgerald. And he probably woke up knowing he would call Jackson back.

Willow didn't like all the intervention Zelda was doing for this project. Because of her, Emma Ross got involved; therefore, Zelda was behind the movie's shift in focus from Scott to Zelda. And now she was apparently responsible for Jackson getting such a quick call back.

Not that he didn't deserve the quick call back, because Willow was sure he did. When she ran through lines with him, she was impressed with how Jackson nailed Scott's speech and mannerisms. It was very difficult to find footage of Scott's voice, but Jackson managed to find a few things where Scott was talking in his clipped, deep midwestern voice. Finding footage of Scott moving around was also difficult, but Jackson also found some of this footage.

At any rate, when Zelda said she felt like she was seeing Scott come back to life when she saw Jackson portray him, Willow knew Jackson had nailed the part. So it wasn't surprising at all that Jackson got a quick call back. Even if Zelda didn't intervene the way she did, Willow knew Jackson would be called back. He just probably wouldn't be called back so quickly.

At the end of the week, it was official. After Jackson did a screen test with Emma Ross, and he nailed that too, it was announced in the trade papers that Jackson Flynn, a name nobody in Hollywood knew, was going to play the part of F. Scott Fitzgerald in a major biopic opposite Emma Ross, the hottest actress in the world.

Jackson was on his way.

Chapter Twenty-Three

Sarah

On the day Sarah accompanied Max to his doctor, and she went back to the hotel room to talk to Ava, Sarah shared her shame at how she was feeling about Max's diagnosis.

"Okay," Sarah said to Ava. "Here's the deal. Max actually has somewhat of a chance to live. And when I say he has a chance to live, I don't mean he has a chance to prolong his life by a matter of months. I mean, he has a chance to go into an old age home at the age of 85, where the music of The Clash, The Pixies and The Smiths will be piped in through the rooms."

Sarah always thought it was humorous, in a way, that the nursing homes of her generation were not going to be playing big-band and 50s sock hop music like the nursing homes of today were playing. Rather, they would be playing the music of their youth, which meant the nursing homes would be playing Green Day, The Police and Nirvana instead of Bill Haley and the Comets or Glenn Miller. The nursing home dances were going to be playing the music of Abba, Donna Summers, Gloria Gaynor, The Bee Gees and The Village People, not the music of Buddy Holly or Benny Goodman.

And there was a chance, however remote, that Max would be one of the elderly people in a future nursing home forming the letters "YMCA" with his arms.

Ava's eyes got wide. "Seriously? I thought he was given only a few months by the doctors in Boston."

"Well, apparently, there's a promising clinical trial curing previously incurable advanced melanoma cases like Max's. Dr. Quan over at UCLA is sponsoring this trial. He says there's a 20% chance, or around there, that Max can be cured."

"That's amazing! I mean, there's still an 80% chance that Max is not going to have a long life, but I thought that the chance of him living out his life expectancy was zero before we came out here. 20% is much better than zero, you have to admit."

Sarah nodded her head. They were sitting on the back patio of their hotel room, which was right on the beach. The sun had not yet set, but the golden glow was getting closer and closer to the outer edge of the water.

"I'm going to confess something to you. Something I'm so ashamed of, and if anybody ever asked me if I felt this way, I would tell them no. They couldn't torture it out of me. But..."

Ava seemed to know what she was thinking. "I understand. You married him when you weren't sober, and if you knew that Max might not be dying, I doubt you would've stayed married to him. You would've gotten it annulled immediately."

Sarah took a deep breath. "Yes. Yes. That's exactly what

the problem is. I mean, if things were normal, and Max wasn't dying, I wouldn't have stayed married to him because I don't know him. But I definitely would've dated him to see where things would go. I was very interested in him romantically. Very attracted to him. But I wouldn't have committed myself to him without knowing more about him."

"Because of Nolan?" Ava asked.

Sarah nodded. "Because of Nolan. You see, I was 30 years old when I met Nolan. And I fell head over heels in love with him. I made the impulsive decision to quit my job and follow him around the world. I didn't know him very well when I made that decision - we had been dating for less than a month at that time."

Ava was nodding her head. "I think I understand where this is going."

"I'm sure you do," Sarah said. "Anyhow, I loved what I knew about him at that time. I loved his intellect, curiosity, and way of looking at the world. It seemed much like my own way of looking at the world. I thought he was compassionate, funny, romantic, and so very sexy. And when he said he spent his professorial breaks traveling around the world, and he wanted me to be by his side when he traveled to places I'd always fantasized about, I didn't even think twice before I said yes."

"And it all went so wrong."

"Yes. It all went so wrong, starting when I took the rap for Lauren's drugs. I saw his true colors then. And I saw what ugliness lay beneath the façade he was displaying to the world. To the world, and to me for the first couple of years, he was this nice, charitable guy who volunteered at a homeless shelter and fostered older dogs who needed homes and probably wouldn't be able to find one because of their age."

That was one of the things that Sarah absolutely loved about Nolan. He habitually went to animal shelters, and if there was a dog who was older than 10 years old, he would offer to foster that dog until the dog found a permanent home. There were several times when the dog would find a permanent home, but there were other times when the dog did not. Several times, Nolan cheerfully provided a home for the senior dogs he fostered until the dog died a natural death.

As for him volunteering for the homeless shelter, he went to the shelter once a month to work the food line. Sarah went along with him when he did this. He also sometimes volunteered his time to stay with homeless families who were living itinerantly in a church-run home over the holidays. That home needed people to provide food, cook and stay overnight, and Nolan volunteered for this every year.

For the first couple of years, when Sarah was dating Nolan, Sarah saw Nolan's good points only. Maybe it was because they were in the heady first days of love. Maybe it was because nothing had tested them so far. Whatever the reason, Sarah really thought Nolan was for her. She didn't even care that they weren't married. She just wanted to be with him.

But when he hung her out to dry for Lauren's drugs, and, worse, he wrote a letter to the architectural board filled with lies about her because he wanted to make sure she couldn't get her architectural license back, Sarah realized the fantasy wasn't true after all. What was true was that Nolan would go to any lengths possible to ensure that Sarah stayed with him.

At that point, when Sarah figured out who Nolan was and how much Nolan didn't care about her, Sarah started to despise him.

Now, here was Max. And Max, like Nolan, seemed to be a very nice guy. It was true that when she first met him, she didn't like him because she felt he was judging her. But once she got to know him, she realized her first impressions were wrong. He had a reason for opposing her for the school board. He had a reason for keeping her at arm's length.

Sarah was starting to warm up to Max when they went to Vegas. But she didn't anticipate marrying him at that time. And, because she was so burned by her extremely impulsive decision to follow Nolan around the world, so much so that she looked back on that decision as the pivotal point in her life, and not in a good way, there was no way she would let an impulsive marriage stand.

It was only because Max offered the possibility to Sarah that she could raise his daughter that Sarah agreed to stay married to him. But what was going to happen if, six months from now, or however long it took for the mono-clonal antibodies to cure Max, if that was going to happen, Max announced to Sarah that he was going to be well?

Ava took Sarah's hand. "Sarah, I understand your dilemma."

"So does Max. He was the one who said that if he was able to live a normal life, he might want to end our marriage. But I don't know if he said that because he wanted to give me an out, or he was the one who was looking for the out."

Sarah and Ava sat silently, watching the waves roll in on the beach for a few moments. At the moment, neither wanted to address the elephant in the room. Should Sarah just annul the marriage now? If she did that, and Max did pass away, she would no longer have a right to Julia. That would leave Julia vulnerable to having to live with her aunt Hannah in New York City, and Julia told Sarah that would be unacceptable to her. Sarah thought that would be unfair to Julia after she promised to take care of her after Max died.

But how weird would it be if, after Max announced he's going to get better, Sarah decided to end the marriage at that point? And did Sarah even want to end the marriage at all? She didn't really know the answer to that question. And maybe she wouldn't ever know it. Maybe she would get sucked into staying married to him because she felt obligated, or even because she fell in love with him. Either way, Sarah was going to go along. If she stayed married to him because she was obligated, she would suppress her feelings, just like she did with Nolan. She became an expert in denying her feelings when she was with Nolan. She might have to do it again if she decided to stay married to Max.

"Well," Ava finally said. "Let's not get ahead of ourselves. We don't know what is going to happen with Max. The treatment might not work. Or it might. I think you need to evaluate where you are once you find out more about what's going to happen with him."

Sarah just nodded her head. Ava was right. She was spinning, when she might not need to be. She had to trust the universe, because the universe knew what was going to be right for her.

That night, around 2 AM, Sarah's dilemma was resolved.

Max had had a massive stroke and had died. Mary called Sarah to tell her this.

Sarah's heart dove to her shoes. It was only then that Sarah understood just what she was secretly hoping for. She was hoping, after all, that Max would get better and that she could stay married to him. She now understood that that was her fantasy, even if she couldn't admit to it - that she could raise Julia with Max by her side.

Shaking, she went over to Ava, who was sleeping in the bed next to Sarah's. The tears started when she told Ava about what had happened, and she thought they would never stop.

Damn. She was prepared for this to happen. This was *supposed* to happen. It was the original reason why Sarah was out in California - to help Max die with dignity. But Dr. Quan had given her hope. He had given him hope, too.

Thank God she didn't tell Julia and Mary about Dr. Quan's news. If she did tell them, they would be just as devastated as she was at that moment.

"Ava," Sarah said, shaking her sister awake.

Ava sat up straight in bed. "What's wrong?" she asked. "What happened?"

"Max," Sarah said, in between heaving sobs. "He's dead. Massive stroke. Ava, I was so ready for this, but now it's here, and I don't think I can take it."

Ava wrapped her arms around Sarah and let her cry on her shoulder. "Sarah, I'm so sorry. I'm so, so, so sorry."

Sarah nodded her head. "Ava, I think I would've stayed married to him. I was afraid of that, because I don't want to get sucked into a toxic situation again. But I think I would've seen it through. I think we could've been very happy together."

"I'm sure you would've been," Ava said. "And Max would've been so lucky to have you as his wife."

"But now we'll never know," Sarah said. "We'll never

know if we could've been that old couple in a couple of rocking chairs on a veranda, talking about the old days and how crazy we were to get married on a whim. We'll never know what it would've been like to raise Julia together. Oh, God, poor Julia."

As Sarah sobbed, she started to confront the enormity of what was about to happen. She was going to be a mother. She was going to move back to California, where she was going to have to start over, yet again. It all sounded like such a good idea, but, all at once, she felt overwhelmed.

There were the logistics - she was going to have to find a house, and she was going to have to be settled in with Julia before the beginning of the school year. She was going to have find a job, hopefully at a winery. She was going to have to find movers. She was going to have to move, and she HATED moving. Hated it with a purple passion.

And there was the reality of the situation - she was going to grieve for Max, and she was going to grieve hard. She was thrown for a loop by the news of his death. And she was going to be dealing with a daughter who had just lost everything. Well, not quite everything, as Julia was going to be close to her aunt Mary. But Julia was going to be dealing with the grief that comes when you suddenly become an orphan.

All this at the tender age of 13. It was going to be a lot to deal with, to say the very least.

As Sarah swallowed hard, she got dressed and went over to Mary's home.

She was going to have to deal with another huge life change.

Tomorrow.

Heartfelt Friendships and New Beginnings

AINSLEY
KEATON

The Malibu
Girls

A SCONSET BEACH NOVEL

vinci-books.com/malibu-girls

**In Malibu, the gang discovers that starting fresh might
lead to unexpected destinies.**

Willow finds herself unexpectedly drawn to Ava's son, Jackson
Flynn, as she immerses herself in writing a screenplay about Zelda
Fitzgerald. Ava navigates the complexities of her attraction to her
stepbrother Elijah while exploring her spiritual side through
Judaism. Hallie flourishes in her new position at a wellness retreat.

Turn the page for a free preview…

The Malibu Girls: Chapter One

Ava

Ava arrived back at Nantucket, determined to try to do something about the house she'd inherited. She'd talked to Sarah at length about the possibility of moving back to California, and she was starting to get excited about the prospect.

Like Sarah, Ava was bored for much of the year in Nantucket. The pace was just too slow, and her business, such as it was, relied upon tourists, which were only prominent for three months out of the year. Everything was hopping from Memorial Day to Labor Day - the bars, the restaurants, the nightlife, the country clubs - everything was going all the time. Her bed and breakfast was always full during the summer months. But after Labor Day, everything quieted down, and everything was so slow that Ava often found herself without something to do. And, for somebody who was used to the fast pace of a large law firm in New York City, boredom was deadly.

When she first moved to Nantucket, it was a welcome respite. Her life in New York City was extremely stressful - she hated working for her law firm because it relied upon shady wealthy people trying to get out of paying their taxes, which appalled Ava. She'd spent so many years working 70 hours a week, so, at first, Nantucket was like an extended vacation. But the town had long since lost its appeal, although she had her best friends and sister there, which made life on the island bearable and sometimes exciting. But now Sarah was going to move to California, along with Quinn, and Ava couldn't think of anything less appealing than staying on the island without two of her anchors.

There were two things she was going to try to do - one, she was going to see what she could do about selling her home there on Nantucket. The terms of the will dictated that she couldn't sell the house for five years, and she'd only been in the house for two. Not even that. So, obviously, if she wanted to sell the house, she was in danger of losing it.

The second thing she wanted to do immediately was to talk to Hallie and see what she thought about the possibility of moving out to California. After all, Hallie was only on Nantucket because Ava and Quinn had moved out there. If Ava and Quinn left the island, along with Sarah, then Hallie wouldn't know anybody on the island aside from Willow.

So, the first thing Ava decided to do was talk to an attorney. Quinn had recommended a woman by the name of Estrella Benton, who was a friend of Quinn's friend, Asher. Asher was somebody Quinn had been tempted to date on several occasions but had decided against it. Things were just not quite right. But Asher was a good friend to Quinn, so she was always in contact with him, and he gave Estrella's name. Estrella lived in Boston, so that's where Ava was headed on the Monday after she got back to Nantucket.

She arrived at Estrella's office, located in a high rise in the heart of Boston. Estrella's office was on the 50th floor, which boded well, in Ava's opinion, because it meant Estrella was probably a successful attorney. The only people who could afford an office on such a high floor were people who did very well in their profession.

Estrella herself came out to greet Ava when Ava got to the office. "Hello, Ava," she said. "Come on in."

Ava followed Estrella to her office, which was all hardwood floors, gleaming corner desks, and eclectic artwork on the wall. Estrella was a bit of an imposing figure, as she was almost 6 feet tall, with long braided hair and beautiful cocoa au lait skin. She spoke with an accent that Ava pinpointed as South African.

Estrella smiled. "How can I help you?"

Ava explained what she was trying to do. She told Estrella all about the will, how she apparently was stuck with the house for the next three years, and how she wanted to sell the house so she could buy something in Malibu.

Estrella nodded her head. "Let me ask you a question. In this case, if you sold the house or otherwise violated the terms of the will conditions, does the document specify who would get the house if you violated the conditions?"

Ava shook her head. "No, it doesn't specify. No alternate heir is named if the will fails because I violated its conditions."

"Well then, the laws of succession would come into play here. Is there a surviving spouse?" the beautiful attorney asked.

Ava thought about Esther, James' wife, and a chill went up her spine. She didn't want to do one thing in the world, and that was to confront Esther about any of this. Ava assumed Esther didn't know about her, even though Morty,

James' best friend from way back, told Ava that her birth was a way of saving their marriage because Esther also had a child out of wedlock.

The situation was that James, the man who willed her the house on Nantucket, had an affair with her mother back in the 1960s when he was married to Esther. Ava was a result of that affair. Ava found this out recently when her mother came clean, and that caused a huge rift between them for a bit. Ava had long since forgiven her mother, but she never wanted to confront James' family.

Esther was still alive. She was in her early 90s, and Ava didn't know much about her other than that she was quite elderly. Ava didn't want to talk to her. She was still ashamed of everything that happened and how her birth came about, even though she didn't need to be. It wasn't her fault. Her mother was the one who had an affair, not her, yet she felt guilty for it all.

Ava nodded her head. "Yes, there is a surviving spouse."

"OK. Are you friendly with the surviving spouse?"

"No. In fact, I've never talked to her. It's very complicated."

"You should probably contact her if you want to do something with the will. There's no way you can avoid the will's terms. What James Bloch did here was a 'Dead Hand' clause. He's trying to control the disposal of his house from beyond the grave. Sometimes these 'Dead Hand' clauses can be void if they're against public policy. An example of this would be a clause where the will is valid only if the benefactor divorces her husband. That would be against public policy because it isn't a good thing to demand a divorce, so that would be one way of getting out of that particular clause. But in your case, there's nothing like that. So the clause is the clause. The only thing you could do is talk to the surviving spouse and see if she could deed the house over to you once she receives it."

Ava felt hopeful that there was a way of disposing of the house. She knew that if she sold the Nantucket house, she could buy a nice house in Malibu. Yet, she wasn't too encouraged about what she had to do to get out from under the terms of the will.

"Tell me how all this will work."

"I'll give a call to the executor of the estate and explain what's happening. Once you sell the house or take a lien against it, the will becomes void and the surviving heir automatically gets the property. And then she could sign the deed to you, so you have the house free and clear. That would be the best approach if you can get her to agree to do that. In fact, that would be the only way you could get out from under the terms of the will."

Ava thought about this approach. She knew one way she could violate the will's terms: ask her mother to take a lien against the house. Ava didn't believe she could actually get a mortgage against the house because any mortgage holder would do a record check, find out the terms of the will, and refuse to give Ava a mortgage. But her mother would do it if she asked her to.

All of this seemed extremely risky, however. She could talk to Esther and ask her if she'd be willing to participate in this transaction. Ava felt she had nothing to lose if she asked her. If she said no, then that was that. Ava would stay in the house or hire somebody to run the place full-time. Jessica, the young lady who had been staying with her in exchange for working around the inn, was also going to move to Los Angeles because Andrew, the musician she was in love with, was moving out to the West Coast to be closer to his recording studios.

So it'd be a matter of Ava finding somebody to run the inn, but that wouldn't be easy. Unfortunately, because the island was so quiet for most of the year, it'd be difficult to find somebody to stay there full-time throughout the year.

After talking with Sarah about the possibility of moving out to California, Ava became excited. But, she was becoming less excited now because it looked like she would have to go ahead and stay in the house after all.

But she wasn't going to go down without a fight. She drew a breath as she thought about the possibility of having to talk to Esther face to face. She would have to meet the woman who was married to Ava's father when Ava was born. The woman who was betrayed by James. She didn't want to open that wound.

But, then again, there was a reasonable assumption that Esther knew all about her. Morty told Ava that since Esther also had a baby out of wedlock, the two mistakes essentially canceled one another out. Because of this, Esther and James could move forward in their marriage. So, the assumption was that Esther knew all about Ava.

She would definitely have to talk to Sarah about what she should do.

Ava thanked Estrella for the advice, paid her, and left.

That evening, Ava hosted Sarah, Quinn, and Hallie at her house. She ordered organic food from an organic restaurant on the island and, of course, had a bottle of wine ready to go. The ladies always liked to get together when they had a pressing need, and today was no exception.

In fact, because of everything that was happening, there was more need than ever for the ladies to come together.

Ava hoped she wasn't making the wrong decision, but she was afraid that she was.

"So, here's the deal," Ava told the ladies. "I need to talk to Esther, James' surviving spouse. I need to ask her if she'd be willing to participate in a transaction where I do something to void the will. She would get the house automatically when I take this action, and then she would just deed me the house once she took possession of it. It's very risky. Because what if she lies to me and says she's going to do it but then doesn't? That would be the worst-case scenario. I mean, if she just said 'no,' my path is set. I'll have to stay here."

It wouldn't be the worst thing in the world, having to stay in this beautiful house on Nantucket. Still, without Quinn and Sarah on the island with her, it would be an empty existence. Ava never appreciated how much she relied upon her posse to keep her spirits up daily. Now, she was faced with two of her anchors moving across the country. The thought made her want to vomit.

It was really true that people need people. And it's not always easy to find your person in life. Ava had yet to find her person in the form of a romantic relationship, but she definitely found her person, or people, with Hallie, Quinn, and Sarah. They were a unit. They were the village for her. If they were going to move to California, then Ava was too.

Besides, she was bored.

So bored.

Sarah understood why Ava was very hesitant to talk to Esther. "Ava, I know what you're getting at. You don't want to talk to Esther because you don't want to drive a stake through her heart. But, then again, you told me Esther knew James had an affair and a child out of wedlock. And she probably knew that that child was you. So, I don't think you have much to worry about. I'm sure she already knows about you, and, for all you know, she'll welcome you with open arms."

"But what if she doesn't? What if she slams the door in my face?" Ava knew the answer to that question before she even asked it. If Esther slammed the door in her face, then she slammed the door in her face. There was nothing that could be done at that point.

"It's worth a shot," Sarah said. "Ava, I'm looking forward to moving to California because I believe that's where I belong. But I'm not looking forward to leaving you behind. I mean, it seems like we've been making up for lost time. I feel closer to you now than I ever have. Things just won't be quite right if you're not out there with me. So, I think you should go ahead and at least try it."

Quinn smiled. "Goes without saying, I agree. I already had my eye on a house out there. I'm thinking about moving to the Venice Beach area. They have such beautiful turn-of-the-century homes, some of them facing canals. I'd be dying to get ahold of one of those older homes and work my magic."

Quinn was referring to some of the big old houses in the Venice Beach area built by a developer named Abbot Kinney in 1905. Kinney wanted to recreate the feel and vibe of Venice, Italy, so he built the canals and the homes that faced these canals. There were quite a few of those old homes because the Venice Beach area seemed to be an older area of town. Ava had visited the Venice Beach area because, when she was with Sarah visiting Mary, the sister of Sarah's now-deceased boyfriend Max, Ava explored the city while Sarah was gone. Mary lived in Malibu, so she and Sarah stayed at a Malibu resort.

The Venice Beach area wasn't far away from the Malibu

area, only about a 10-minute drive, and she went there one evening to catch the vibe and see how things were out there.

It seemed to be a very lively area of town. On the beach was a spinning class of about 50 people with glowing head-phones. On the grassy area, around 100 young people with glowing sticks were having a dance party. There were bars and restaurants right on the beach and they all seemed to be hopping. And, because it was California, Ava thought the nightlife on Venice Beach was probably hopping all year round, unlike here on Nantucket. And all through the beach were little enclaves with chairs and people hanging around. It seemed like a fun, lively atmosphere, and Ava thought it'd be a nice place for Quinn to settle with her young daughter.

Just down the street from the beach was the Santa Monica pier, another lively place to go. The Santa Monica pier was like a mini carnival, with musicians, magicians, face painters, artists, and seafood restaurants up and down the pier. The Santa Monica pier was a place where people liked to gather in the evenings, as the sunset behind the Santa Monica hills provided the backdrop to Santa Monica and Malibu.

Ava thought living in the Venice Beach or Santa Monica areas would be a good idea. But she also loved the homes that were part of the Malibu Lagoon State Beach. She went hiking along the little trail there, admiring the beautiful sycamore, pine and pepper trees that grew wild around the lagoon, and she was more than impressed with the homes that were right on the beach. These homes were, like the Venice Beach area, older, although they didn't seem as old as the Venice Beach houses. Most of them were probably built around the 1940s or 1950s, and they sported huge decks that jetted out of the homes. The water came all the way up to the retaining walls that all the homes had to keep the surf away from their buildings.

Ava thought if she lived in Malibu, it would be the best of both worlds - she could still sit on her deck and listen to the waves rolling in every night. And that was something she'd gotten used to there on Nantucket. Her favorite time of the day was when she could sit on her deck, close her eyes and hear the surf coming in. She'd miss that if she didn't have it.

However, with the Malibu Lagoon State Beach homes, she'd still be able to hear the surf rolling in from her window or deck, and she could just relax. At the same time, it was close enough to the liveliness of the Santa Monica Pier and the Venice Beach areas that she could enjoy the liveliness and nightlife of those areas when she felt like it.

"Quinn, I agree that the beautiful older homes on Venice Beach would be perfect for you. With your interior decorating eye, you could make one of those houses shine like a diamond."

Ava would have also loved to get a house on Venice Beach, but she couldn't find one that was right on the beach like they had in Malibu. That was the only reason why Malibu was a much more attractive prospect for her than the Venice Beach area.

Sarah took a deep breath. "I'm really looking forward to moving out to California, too. It's a bit of a shame because I just bought the house here. But, I already have a few offers to buy my house for $2.5 million, which is much more than what I paid. So I'll be able to get a nice little bungalow out in California. I won't be able to afford anything as nice as what you're going to get, Ava, assuming you can get out from under your house here. But I think I can find a home in the Venice Beach area that would be in my price range.

And I'm looking forward to maybe finding a job at a winery. They have quite a few up in the Santa Monica hills. I visited them while I was out there."

Ava had also visited the wineries in the Santa Monica hills. Ava had to admit it was a bit scary that a winery was high in those hills. To get to the winery, she had to drive up a lot of very windy roads that went straight up a mountain. Many of those roads didn't even have the semblance of a guardrail. And, to make things even more dangerous, people tended to tailgate drivers out there. Ava thought that wine tasting and driving down those hills didn't go hand in hand. She shuddered to think about driving drunk, misjudging a curve and sailing down the ravine.

Yet, she thought the winery she'd visited was a beautiful one. It was a very hot day when they went there, unseasonably warm, considering it was only April. She had a glass of wine while looking over the panoramic views afforded by being so high in the hills. The winery had all different kinds of cabernets and merlots and chablis. Ava drank a bit too much, and since she was driving, she had to hang out there for several hours until she sobered up. It was a beautiful evening, and Ava thought this winery would be a perfect place for Sarah to land.

Sarah and Ava had even talked about the possibility of buying their own winery. That was actually the goal.

Ava wasn't clear about what she would do once she got to Malibu. She had experience running a bed and breakfast, and she had experience as a lawyer. However, she'd long since decided that law was not for her. So she and Sarah had fantasized one night while they were in California about buying a winery in the Santa Monica hills. That was something Ava could possibly do if she made enough money off the sale of her Nantucket house. They could even get their mother to get in on the deal. Their mother was still a judge in Boston, but she was always looking for investment opportunities. She originally had invested in Ava's bed and breakfast on Nantucket. In fact, without her investment, Ava probably wouldn't have been able to have opened up. Or, at least, she wouldn't have been able to have the luxury she had there on Nantucket. So, her mother helped her. However, once Ava and her mother, Colleen, made up and decided they'd have a true mother and daughter relationship from that point on, Colleen told Ava she didn't want any of the profits from her bed and breakfast. That showed Ava she was ready to move on in their relationship and become closer.

But, if Ava and Sarah were going to ask Colleen to invest in the winery, they'd make sure it was much more of a business relationship. They imagined Colleen would be a silent partner in this endeavor.

Of course, at the moment, this was all pipe dreams. But it was something Ava was allowing herself to dream about. She'd absolutely love to be in business with her sister. And she wanted more than anything for Sarah to have a substantial position. At the moment, Sarah was just working for Ava as a sommelier. Sarah was perfectly happy doing that, but Ava knew Sarah could be so much more. She could do so much more with her life. And owning a winery would be something that could really challenge Sarah and make her happy. Ava wanted that for her sister.

Of course, all of this turned to whether Ava could sell her home there on Nantucket.

Hallie was quiet for a little bit. Ava knew Hallie would end up coming out to California with them, but she was a little hesitant about what she would do when she got out there. She was trying to make a name for herself in the life coaching realm. She had a few clients there on Nantucket. One of them was an artist by the name of Conrad, who was very prominent, and Hallie had a thing for him. Hallie also helped Ava's daughter, Charlotte, when Charlotte was trying to figure out her life. Hallie had battled breast cancer, but the last time she went for a checkup, she was informed she was cancer free.

"What's going on, Hallie?" Ava asked her. "What are you thinking?"

Hallie started to laugh. "Well, it turns out that Morgan, her wife, Emma Claire, and their new adopted child, Zendaya, are moving to Los Angeles. The art gallery business in San Francisco is a little on the wane. I guess many of the San Francisco artists are moving down to Los Angeles because that's where the new art scene is. Morgan and Emma Claire are going to buy a home in Los Angeles and raise their child there. But I don't want her thinking I'm following her again."

That was one thing that Hallie always worried about. When Morgan was young, Hallie latched on to her and tried to make Morgan's life her own. That was because, at that time, Hallie didn't really have a life to speak of. She was married to a very toxic man and wasn't working outside the home. So, when Morgan started to branch out a little, working at an art gallery as a curator, Hallie tried to ride her coattails. Hallie volunteered for a job at the same art gallery. She made a pest of herself, so much so that the gallery owner told her not to come around anymore. And then, when Morgan moved across the country to San Francisco, Hallie felt it was because she was overbearing.

But things were very good between Hallie and Morgan these days. And part of the reason why was because they lived across the country from one another. Morgan came to visit Hallie from time to time, and Hallie did the same for Morgan. Hallie worried that the same toxic codependency relationship would emerge again if they lived in the same city.

Ava put her arm around Hallie. "Hallie, don't worry about it. You're a different person than you were when she was growing up. You're no longer in that same relationship with your husband. You're making a life for yourself. You're working on getting your nutrition counseling license. You're becoming a life coach. You're not the same woman who didn't know who she was and where she was going. So you're not going to be the same person who smothers Morgan."

"I know what you're saying, but I'm afraid Morgan will think I'm out there because of her. She just moved out there. She just opened up a new gallery out there." Hallie shook her head. "The last thing I want to happen is I start smothering her without even thinking about it, and she pulls away from me. I mean, it's going to be good to be in the same city as her, don't get me wrong. I just have to watch myself and ensure I don't make her feel like I'm hovering."

To be honest, Ava worried about the same thing with Jackson. Jackson was her son and an actor in Los Angeles who just got a major part in a major movie opposite the biggest A-list actress in the world, Emma Ross. Ava worried about Jackson constantly. Before he got this part, she worried he wouldn't make it in Hollywood. He was doing quite well with the modeling business. Acting, not so much. And, now that he got this major part in this major movie, Ava worried he wouldn't do well. Maybe the movie wouldn't do well, or critics would savage him, and he would never make another movie again. That happened to quite a few people over the years. They were unknown, they had a big movie, the movie flopped, and they were never heard from again. It was so much pressure on her son, Ava just couldn't stand it. So Ava worried that she, too, would smother her son.

"Sugar, you're going to be fine," Quinn said to Hallie. "Things are going very well for you and Morgan. And, you have your best friends around you. We'll make sure that you don't go overboard with her."

The ladies listened to the surf and drank their wine. It was a beautiful evening in April. The island would start gearing up again in a few more weeks for the summer rush. Ava's inn would be filled to the brim with people and a waiting list.

But Ava hoped that by the end of the month, she would be selling her house and heading out to California.

The Malibu Girls: Chapter Two

Ava

Ava had nervously made an appointment to see Esther Bloch. The older lady was still living in New York City. Brooklyn, to be exact.

When Ava called Esther, she was amazed that Esther knew exactly who she was and, in fact, was eager to speak with her. So, that was a huge relief for Ava. She imagined that Esther would slam the phone down on her when she called her. And, if Esther slammed the phone down on her, Ava would figure she deserved it.

Instead, Esther spoke warmly on the phone. "Sure, I'll meet with you. To tell you the truth, I've always been curious about you. I've never had the guts to actually call you myself. I figured that you probably didn't want to talk to me. And, I also had it in my head that maybe you didn't know the truth about your father. But I guess you do know the truth about my James. So, sure, I'd love to meet you."

So Ava found herself flying into New York City and

heading across the bridge to Brooklyn. Her heart was in her throat after she called her Uber and found herself heading toward Esther's home. Yes, Esther was extremely friendly with her on the phone. But meeting her face to face would be a completely different story. And she also was going to find out more about her half-siblings. There were two other daughters - Rachel and Deborah - along with a son who had a different father from James. That son's name was Elijah, and he was the only one in the Bloch family with no blood relation to Ava. Elijah was about Ava's age.

There also was another daughter who was murdered - Valerie. She was Jessica's mother.

Ava found that she was actually looking forward to possibly meeting Rachel, Deborah, and even Elijah. Rachel and Deborah had the same father as Ava, so they were her half-sisters. Ava was looking forward to learning more about that part of her family tree.

Ava got to Esther's home and knocked on the door. It was a beautiful brownstone with bay windows and was built probably around 1900 or so. The neighborhood was quiet and treelined, the kind of neighborhood that Ava always loved to visit during the autumn months because the spectacular foliage gave these streets a kind of glow. Like a typical Brooklyn neighborhood, the brownstones were interspersed with coffee shops, delis, restaurants, and a bar here and there.

After she knocked on the door, a man answered it. Ava deduced the guy was the butler by his demeanor.

"Hello," he said in a very formal manner. "You must be Ava Flynn. Esther is waiting for you in the parlor."

The man led Ava back through the house to a room in the back that must have been the parlor. The brownstone was beautiful - high ceilings, chandeliers, hardwood floors, and the beautiful old crown molding that Ava always admired in these older homes. The brownstone was fronted by an enormous bay window with three panels and a cushion.

Ava arrived at the parlor and saw a tiny woman sitting in a high-backed chair next to the fireplace. She was wearing glasses that she lowered to the end of her nose to get a closer look at Ava.

She nodded her head and then stood up. "Ava Flynn. At long last, we meet."

She extended her hand, and Ava shook it. As she shook Esther's hand, she looked at her own hand and saw it was shaking like a leaf. "I'm so sorry. I'm just really nervous about meeting you."

At that, Esther started to laugh heartily. "Goodness. I've always felt the same way about you. I've known about you since the beginning, you know."

Ava's nodded. "That's what I understand," she said.

Esther shook her head. "That was a really bad time in our marriage. I know you've met with Morty, so I know you know the broad contours about what happened. I was caring for my sick mother here in New York, and I met a man while I was here in New York City. His name was Michael Steiner. We had a brief fling, and I had a child with him. And around the same time, James was having an affair with your mother, and he fathered you with her. We weren't speaking at that time, James and me. When I met Michael, I fell head over heels in love with him. I didn't even think about James in Cambridge, who was waiting for me to come home. But then, after I got pregnant with Elijah, I realized I didn't want to be with Michael. I realized my husband, James, was who I belonged with. He was who I took vows with. My mother passed away while I was caring for her, and after that, I returned to James."

Ava quietly listened to her. It seemed that Esther wanted to unburden herself about what happened during that time.

"And you were pregnant with Elijah when you returned to him?"

"Yes. And I had to tell him about it. It was the hardest thing I've ever done, looking the man I love in the eye and telling him I was pregnant with another man's child. And he reacted to my story very calmly. It turns out he had the same secret he was afraid to tell me about - he had fathered a child with your mother, Colleen."

Esther looked out the window, her rheumy blue eyes getting misty. Ava instinctively wanted to hug the woman, but she didn't really know her, so she put her hand on hers.

Esther finally just shook her head. "What a mess we got ourselves into. But we decided we were going to go and see a marital counselor. There was so much hurt between us. So much pain, so much rage that was coursing through our marriage. We had so many hurtful words that we had said to one another that just couldn't be taken back. But the marital counselor was able to put us on a good footing. And I know if I'd returned to James pregnant with another man's child, he would've rightfully told me to turn around and leave the house if he didn't make the same mistake himself. Because he made the same mistake I did, having an affair, thinking that affair was going to somehow fix the hole inside both of our souls, we could go forward and forgive one another. It was so difficult. It was years of counseling. Twice a week counseling. But we were able to rebuild our marriage, brick by brick, day by day, second by second. And, about five years after Elijah and you were born, we turned a corner. We fell back in love. We felt like we did when we first got married."

Her eyes were now getting misty, and she shook her head. Ava's heart went out to her, for it was obvious that Esther really missed her James, the love of her life and her husband for over 65 years.

"I always was grateful for you," Esther said. "Because of your birth, I was able to have 65 years with the man I loved. And if you were never born, I probably would've been divorced from my James in 1968 or somewhere around there. I would've never gotten those extra 50-odd years with my James."

Esther looked at the needlepoint she was working on when Ava first entered the parlor. Her hands were that of a woman over 90 - wrinkled, with fine skin, brown spots and blue veins showing through. Her blue eyes were cloudy. Yet, she had the posture of a much younger woman. She sat perfectly straight in her chair. She was a proud woman, Ava could tell. And how humiliating it must've been for her to admit to James about Elijah.

"Esther, thank you for telling me this story. I know I got some of the story from Morty like you say. But it really means a lot to hear it from you. And I'm so sorry all this happened to you and James."

Esther shook her head. "Dear, please don't say that. Elijah has been a light in my life. He's such a good man. He's a doctor. He's saved countless lives in Africa when he worked with Doctors Without Borders. I couldn't imagine what the world would be like without him. So, I can never regret having him. I could never regret the affair I had with his father. Because without that affair, there would be no Elijah. And without Elijah, all the people he saved might not have been. It's like that movie, *It's a Wonderful Life*. In that movie, George Bailey's life touched so many other lives. Without his birth, his brother would have died, and the druggist would have been in prison. And his brother saved a lot of people himself. It's just like the butterfly theory. That butterfly floats his wings, and the repercussions go on forever. In this case, the repercussions were amazing. No, the world is a much better place because Elijah is in it."

Ava wondered if Esther thought about having a pregnancy termination when she discovered she was pregnant with Elijah. Ava thought that was probably what she would've done. If she got pregnant with another man's child while she was married and she thought that the birth would be the end of the marriage, she probably would've gotten an abortion to keep the pregnancy secret from her husband.

Of course, Ava was never going to ask Esther that question. But Esther seemed to know what she was thinking.

"I thought about it, you know. Terminating. Of course, back then, it wasn't so easy to do. Abortion wasn't legal everywhere. It wasn't legal in New York at that time. New York didn't legalize it until 1970. Even in Massachusetts, abortion was only legal when the mother's life was threatened. Of course, I was a woman of means. I was married to the son of a very wealthy man. I could have gone overseas to have it done. But, then again, that would involve my telling James, which defeated the purpose of getting an abortion. But, believe me, I prayed about it every night. I was so afraid that he would tell me the marriage was over when I told him the truth about Elijah. But I'm so glad I had the courage to tell him. And we had the courage to move forward."

Esther had a smile on her face that made Ava feel very warm inside. This older lady had so much love in her heart, that was obvious. And she seemed to even have a love for

Ava. She'd just met Ava, but then again, she knew about her for all these years. So, maybe she had developed an affection for the idea of Ava long ago.

"I'm very happy for you and James," Ava said. "It's wonderful to find a great love. And it's even better to really fight for that love." Ava thought about Daniel, the love of her life. What she wouldn't give for the opportunity to have fought for him. But he died in a car accident right before the birth of the triplets. She also thought about Christopher, the husband who cleaned out her bank account. Christopher tried to come back to her, but Ava wasn't having it. Ironically, Christopher fathered a child with another woman while he was married to Ava. He actually married that other woman, making him a bigamist. But Ava didn't really care about that, because she had long stopped caring about Christopher as a romantic relationship. So she could take the stunning news that he had a second family at one time in stride.

"Yes, dear," Esther said. "James was the love of my life. I was so foolish when I met Michael Steiner. I was 35 years old, barely a baby, now that I think about it. Of course, when you get to my age, everybody seems like a baby to you. Even you. I look at you right now, and you seem so young to me. But, I was 35, my mother was dying, and I was just in a very bad state when I met Michael. That's all I could think about. I mistook his affection for me for love. And love was what I desperately needed at that time. James was pulling away from me, and with my mother dying, I was so lost."

Ava's heart went out to the older lady. It was clear that, like her own mother, Esther had so many regrets. But one of those regrets was a beautiful thing, Elijah. It was just how things were supposed to be, probably. If Ava believed in the concept of fate, that everything happened for a reason, she thought that was probably the case here. Elijah was meant to be born, and that was that.

Esther finally took a deep breath. "Now, you are here for a reason. I kind of understood that when you called me. I know you probably were curious about me like I've always been curious about you. But I know that you're here for some other reason."

She raised her eyebrows at Ava, and Ava briefly lost her voice.

"Yes," she said to Esther. "Yes, I am here for a reason."

Ava told Esther all about the will and the conditions. "And, since you're the surviving spouse, you're his closest heir. So, if I do something to void my gift, you'll automatically get the property. So, I'd like to do something to violate the will so that you'll get the property. And then, after you get the property, I'd like you to deed it to me. Free and clear."

Esther nodded her head. "Is that all? Dear, when you called me, I knew you wanted something. And, to be honest with you, whatever you were going to ask me, within reason, I would have given to you. I always felt that you got a raw deal, never knowing your actual father. And, it was my idea to put you into James' will. Well, not really. James was going to always put you into his will, but he wasn't going to necessarily give you that house. We talked about it, and I gave him the idea that you might enjoy that house. And it's worth a lot of money. I want you to have it. I didn't want James to put the stipulations in the will that you had to stay in there for five years. I thought that was excessive. But he wanted you to enjoy the house and feared that you'd just sell the house immediately. I think he wanted you to give Nantucket a chance. He always loved it there. That was his favorite place to go, that house. And then he let our granddaughter, Jessica, live there while recovering from her drug addiction. But he always loved that home."

Esther seemed to take a deep breath.

"So, you'll be willing to participate in this transaction?"

"Of course. As I said earlier, I would have lost James if it weren't for your birth. I know that. He would have never forgiven me for having a child with somebody else if he didn't make the same mistake at the same time. So I always thought you were why I spent so many years with the man I loved so much. So, yes, I would be happy to do anything for you."

"And your daughters, Rachel and Deborah? And your son, Elijah? They won't be upset that you're just going to deed the house to me, free and clear?"

"Dear, what if I said the word no. What would you do?"

"I would stay in the house until the five years were up."

"There's your answer. If I turned you down, you would just keep the house. Either way, none of my children would actually get the house. So they don't even have to know about this transaction, to be honest with you. I'll admit that Rachel was slightly upset you got that house. She always loved that house. But she wasn't too upset about it. She lives in a beautiful condo on the Upper West Side, and she's doing very well for herself. And she has a beach house in the Hamptons. So does Deborah. Elijah has a beach house, too, in Malibu."

"So, all your children have beach houses?"

"Yes. My husband had quite a few properties around the country and ensured that all of our children were taken care of. As for me, I'm perfectly happy here in this brownstone. I don't much like the beach. I never did. Too hot, too sandy, and I have very fair skin, so I would get really horrible sunburns. My kids always loved the beach, but I never did. So, I have no desire to have that house on Nantucket, either. Don't worry. You're not going to be stepping on anybody's toes by taking this house free and clear. Just tell me what I need to do, and I will do it."

"OK. Then I'll go ahead and get my lawyer to draw up the paperwork, contact the executor, and explain what's happening. I need to have my mother take out a small lien against the house, which would void the bequest. Once the bequest is voided, it's just a matter of the executor putting the house into your name, and then you would just transfer the deed to me."

Esther started to laugh. "Oh my goodness, so much cloak and dagger. Well, that's OK. I'll be happy if you get the house at the end of all this rigamarole. And you don't have to worry about staying on that tiny island much longer. By the way, where do you plan on moving to?"

"Ironically enough, I'm going to look at beach houses in Malibu. So, maybe when I get out to California, I can give my stepbrother Elijah a call. Do you think he'd mind?"

Ava thought getting to know her stepbrother was a good idea. She was hungry for information about her father, James, and Elijah would be able to supply that for her. And it was so convenient that he happened to be living out in Malibu, where Ava would hopefully get a house now that she could sell her Nantucket house.

"No, dear, I think he'd love to talk to you," Esther said.

Ava spent most of the afternoon talking with Esther. Esther gave her a lot of good insight about her father, James, and Ava was so grateful that she did this. She was not just grateful because, of course, she'd be able to sell her Nantucket home and establish a new life out in California. The thought of moving out there and hopefully opening up a winery with Sarah excited her. And it also excited her that she could enjoy year-round sunshine and warm weather. She was getting very tired of the harsh winters in this north-eastern town, and she had only experienced the winters not even two times. But she'd lived in New York before she came to Nantucket, so harsh winters had been a thing that she had just had to live with. But now, maybe she wouldn't have to. And that excited her very much.

After she left Esther's home and got in her Uber, she smiled.

California, here I come!

Grab your copy...
vinci-books.com/malibu-girls

About the Author

Ainsley Keaton lives with her hubby and two fur-babies in Southern California. When she's not binge-watching *Grace and Frankie*, *Succession* and *Downton Abbey*, she's reading historical and women's fiction and scouring the beach for sea glass and sand dollars.

Thanks for reading!